Red Rock Crossing

The San Tomas river is in flood and a mixed bunch of travellers is forced to stay in the decaying township of Red Rock Crossing. There is Jesse Grant a once-successful rancher who is fleeing his enemies, the Santos brothers. Then there are Ben and Marty, a pair of Texas Rangers escorting Hamel, a captured outlaw. A hired assassin named Missouri Sam is also waiting to ply his murderous trade and only one man knows his identity.

Ben and his girl Jane, who lives at the crossing, find themselves engaged in a struggle for survival as the town erupts in murder and violence. At last the flood subsides but a mystery must still be unravelled before Missouri pays for his crimes.

Red Rock Crossing

Greg Mitchell

A Black Horse Western

ROBERT HALE · LONDON

© Greg Mitchell 2007
First published in Great Britain 2007

ISBN 978-0-7090-8419-8

Robert Hale Limited
Clerkenwell House
Clerkenwell Green
London EC1R 0HT

The right of Greg Mitchell to be identified as
author of this work has been asserted by him
in accordance with the Copyright, Designs and
Patents Act 1988

Typeset by
Derek Doyle & Associates, Shaw Heath
Printed and bound in Great Britain by
Antony Rowe Limited, Wiltshire

ONE

The confrontation came as a surprise to both parties. Texas Ranger Ben Lawton was walking out of a general store in the small town of Sawpit Flat and literally bumped into Eric Hamel, a wanted bank robber who was about to enter. Recognition was mutual and reactions were swift.

Hamel had sworn never to be taken alive and the ranger knew that within a very short space of time, one of them could be dead.

Ben had a parcel containing a couple of new shirts in his right hand and he thrust this in Hamel's face before letting it go to grab for his gun. The outlaw's revolver was out of its holster when the ranger seized it by the cylinder with his left hand and struggled to keep the muzzle pointing away from him. Hamel was equally as quick and caught Ben's gun hand as he drew his weapon. Just in time the ranger twisted sideways and a knee aimed for his groin struck his thigh instead. He retaliated with a head butt to his opponent's whiskered face. Hamel cursed, snorted blood from his nose and tried to bite his adversary's face but Ben twisted his head away in time.

For an instant they strained against each other but neither man had the advantage The outlaw was a bigger man but his opponent was younger with equal strength and faster reflexes. Both knew that the first one to get his gun pointed in the right direction would win the struggle. Then luck swung the ranger's way. Though he dared not look he could feel that Hamel's gun was a Smith & Wesson Schofield. He moved his fmgers slightly, felt the barrel catch and pressed it. To his great relief he felt the barrel and cylinder move out of alignment with the standing breech. Releasing his hold on the temporarily useless revolver, Ben threw the hardest left hook of his career. It landed heavily right on the point of Hamel's chin snapping his head sideways and sending him spinning away and causing him to lose his grip on the ranger's gun barrel. By the time the dazed man hit the ground, Ben had his Colt trained on him.

'Don't move, Hamel,' he panted. 'There's a sheriff up in Amarillo who's rather keen to meet you.'

The man who had sworn never to be taken alive had a sudden change of heart when looking down the bore of a Colt .45. The determination on the face of the dark-haired young man behind the gun was unspoken evidence that the ranger was prepared to pull the trigger. Slowly Hamel raised both hands.

The next day, Ben and his partner Marty Davis, rode north with the sullen prisoner being led on another horse. The sooner Hamel was delivered to the appropriate authorities, the easier the lawmen would breathe. The Hamel gang had lost a few members in a recent foray against a bank that was not as easy to rob as they had thought, but they were still dangerous. Fearing a rescue attempt by some gang members who remained at large, the rangers chose an out-of-the-way route through rough, remote country for the long ride to Amarillo.

Marty's tanned face, with its drooping, sandy moustache, wrinkled into a smile as he laughingly questioned Ben's choice of routes: 'You wouldn't be going via Red Rock Crossing to see Jane Shelley by any chance?'

'Of course not,' his partner said hastily although that idea had occurred to him. At twenty-five Ben was a year younger than Marty but considered himself years behind in worldly experience although he had been longer as a ranger. He was sticking to a subject he knew when he said, 'Gus Martin and Joe Owens are still on the loose. They would know by now that we have Hamel and chances are they'll be watching the main road looking for a chance to bust him free.'

The lawmen and their prisoner left Sawpit Flat before daylight in the hope of being unobserved. It was a three-day ride to Amarillo.

Then the rain started.

*

Mules do not like mud and it took all of Jesse Grant's efforts to keep the pair in his buckboard moving along the rain-lashed trail that led to Red Rock Crossing. He dared not stop. He needed to be across the San Tomas River before the floods came down. If he timed things right, the floods would be to his advantage. He would be able to cross and lose his pursuers, but he was in a death trap if the floods stopped him on the south side of the stream.

There was a time when this powerfully built, middle-aged man would not have needed to run. His grim face with its cold blue eyes and the hand hovering over his gun butt, had intimidated many a man. As added insurance he had employed a crew of gunfighters when his career was at its zenith. But then he lost a long and bloody range war and things changed. One by one, his gun-toting associates had gone. Some had fled the state; a few were in prison; some had died by the gun. In his bid to become the territory's most powerful cattle baron, he had made many enemies. Now his empire had collapsed along with the political influence he had once been able to call on and his enemies, unforgiving men with long memories, were circling him like wolves around a sick buffalo. Originally he had hoped that he would be allowed to depart peacefully when he lost the range war, but the winners were bent on revenge. He knew for sure that the Santos brothers were on his trail and there would be others as well. Grant had been ruthless in his rise to power and none knew better than he that the people he had often terrorized were unlikely to forgive and forget.

The rain was cascading from the brim of his sodden hat and that shed by his slicker was draining onto his boots so that his feet were cold and wet. He hoped that the canvas wrapping was keeping the water out of the few possessions he was carrying in the tray of the buckboard. They were all he could salvage and would be useful when he started again somewhere else – if he lived long enough.

The buckboard's wheels were sinking lower as the trail became more sodden, increasing the load on the already tired mules, but their owner would not allow them to rest until they were safely across the San Tomas. He figured that the river would be less than an hour's journey away when he looked behind and saw the three riders. They were half a mile back moving slowly, men and horses with heads bent low as the wind-driven rain beat into their faces.

Fear came with a rush. Alone and unguarded for the first time in many years, the former cattle baron wondered if he would ever reach the dubious safety of the crossing. He knew that if his enemies caught him alone, they would try to kill him and the odds were that they would succeed. The best he could hope for was that he could take a few of his attackers to the grave with him. Grant's hands trembled as he cranked a round into the chamber of the Winchester rifle taken from under his seat and undid a couple of buttons on his slicker to allow easier access to his long-barrelled Colt revolver. If the distant riders were the Santos brothers, he could not let them catch up with him. His best hope for survival was to get across the San Tomas River and defend the crossing until the rising floodwaters made it impassable. But to do that meant staying ahead of the riders until he reached town. It took a great effort of will to refrain from trying to whip more speed from the team but he knew that such action might also cause the mules to jib. Instead he shook the reins and urged on the animals with his voice.

Ben reined in his blaze-faced chestnut gelding when he saw the buckboard in the distance. He turned to his companions and said, 'Looks like we're catching up with that buckboard that's been ahead of us for hours.'

Marty peered through the ears of his tall, black mare and warned, 'Let's hang back a bit, we're nearly at the crossing and that *hombre* could be nervous,' He looked at Hamel sitting miserably on a weedy bay mustang. 'He might think we are some of your friends, Eric. We wouldn't want him to take fright and start shooting. Folks get a mite nervous sometimes when they see strange riders coming up behind them.'

Neither ranger was happy about the rain. Both feared that if they were stopped on the south bank of the San Tomas, Hamel's men might be able to find them and attempt a rescue.

'You know this area better than we do,' Marty said to the prisoner. 'What do you reckon our chances are of getting over the river at Red Rock?'

Hamel was in an evil mood and just muttered an obscenity under his breath. In handcuffs with his horse being led, he had no intention of aiding the rangers. Like his captors, he, too, was worried about the depth of the river at Red Rock Crossing but for a different reason.

Red Rock Crossing was never a pretty town, even when it was new. Situated just out of flood reach in a deep canyon, it was mostly a collection of houses and a few business premises arranged facing the river. The road divided the town into two halves. The north side had a saloon, a cantina, and a couple of small businesses and tradesmen's workshops.

The south side had once been the better side with a hotel and a collection of houses. But now the town was dying and some of the residences were already abandoned and had fallen into ruins.

Hiram Waldren stood under the veranda of the faded, weatherboard building bearing the name of the Red Rock Hotel. He was a small man with an untidy grey beard and small, dark eyes that gave him a furtive look. His nose at some time had been badly broken and a long scar showed above the whiskers on his left cheek His faded black coat and trousers were stained in places by the ubiquitous red mud. A hundred yards away, between the high banks, a roaring torrent of foaming brown water was sweeping trees, dead livestock and debris downstream. Nobody in his right mind would try the ford under such conditions.

At the sound of a light footstep beside him, the little man turned to see Jane Shelley who, with her parents, ran the hotel. She was a beautiful girl, not tall but exquisitely formed with a pretty face, long, dark hair and bright blue eyes that seemed to be always smiling. There was a kindness in her soft features that belied the brisk manner she adopted when working about the family business. Some said that such beauty was wasted in Red Rock Crossing, but she seemed happy enough. Since her father had recently broken his leg in a riding accident, Jane did much of the hotel's management while her mother supervised the eating arrangements. All twenty years of her life had been spent at Red Rock Crossing and she had seen the San Tomas in all its moods.

'I don't think anyone will be crossing the river today, Reverend,' she said. 'It's bad for travellers, but could be good for business.'

Waldren pointed to the long, low building on the other side of the road. 'I fear that Dawson's establishment will profit more than yours. With all this rain it is hard to imagine people being thirsty but some become too much so for their own good, I'm afraid. It's almost impossible to make such people see reason.'

Jane laughed. 'Hank Dawson would be a challenge for you, Reverend.'

'He would at that,' the little man admitted. 'But first I must concentrate my efforts on those who want to hear my message. Dawson would not let me through the door of his saloon even if I wanted to enter. From the little I have seen of him, he's a hard and Godless man.'

They were still talking when Grant drove his buckboard into the street. He halted the weary team in front of the hotel. Raising his hat to Jane, he said, 'Howdy, ma'am. Would you know the state of the crossing?'

'You have no chance of getting across, mister. There's about twelve feet of water over the ford and the river's a hundred yards wide.'

Grant's frown deepened. That was the news he had least wanted to hear. He would have to try another course of action. 'I'm a stranger here. Do you have a sheriff or a peace officer of some kind?'

Jane shook her head. 'I'm sorry. The Texas Rangers look in here occasionally, but we have no regular lawman. This town is dying and we no longer have the population to support one.'

'Can anyone else help?' Waldren asked.

'Not unless they're good with a gun, they can't. I have three riders on my tail and they're not far behind. I reckon they're out to kill me. It might be best if you get inside, miss, because there could be a bit of shooting in a minute. They're not getting me

13

without a fight.'

'Surely we should not need to resort to gunplay,' Waldren protested.

'Try telling that to the Santos brothers,' Grant snapped. 'They've sworn to kill me but I won't make it easy for the—' Just in time he remembered he was in the presence of a lady.

As he spoke, Grant looked back along the trail and saw three riders just topping the hill where the road led down to the crossing. Briefly, panic showed in his face but then he set his jaw, grabbed his Winchester and looked around for a good defensive position.

'They're here – best get inside, ma'am.'

Jane looked up the road and laughed. 'You can relax, mister. I know that horse with the white face. Its rider is a Texas Ranger. You have your lawman after all.'

Grant's shoulders sagged in relief as the tension went out of his body.

'You must have been praying mighty hard, my friend,' Waldren told him cheerfully.

'I make my own luck,' Grant said harshly, 'and when things go wrong I don't expect no angel to suddenly appear and get me out of trouble.'

The little man in black looked slightly disappointed but said nothing more.

'That's Ben Lawton, for sure,' Jane told them and hoped that the excitement in her voice did not show. 'You could not want a better man on your side.' She did not say that the young ranger's visits to Red Rock

Crossing had increased in number since they first met a year before, or that her opinion of him might not have all been related to his ability as a lawman.

Marty saw the girl on the veranda and glanced sideways at Ben. 'Looks like your girl's got herself a couple of new admirers,' he said with a knowing smile on his face.

'I don't own her,' Ben muttered defensively. 'She's free to choose any man she wants. Don't you go saying anything to embarrass her.'

Marty loved teasing Ben. 'She's free to choose any man as long as he's a Texas Ranger with a white-faced horse and a fancy six-shooter with an ivory butt.'

Ben's Colt was a presentation weapon given to him by the grateful citizens of a town he had rid of a troublesome element and his partner took great delight in telling him that it was a dude's pistol.

Ben took the bait. When it came to Jane, he always did. 'You're just jealous, Marty, because you don't have a girl.'

'I'm not ready yet for some female to get her hooks into me,' Davis said knowingly. 'Hell, Ben, you need to be careful about women. Just when you reckon they're eating out of your hand, they kick without even laying back their ears. They're all the same. Don't get overconfident.'

Tony Santos looked at the buckboard tracks and chuckled. He was a big man with the dark features of his Mexican father, as harsh and unforgiving as the country in which he had spent most of his life. He was not usually given to humour, but today was feeling good despite the discomfort of riding in the rain. 'It looks like Grant has left us a good clear track to follow,' he said. 'He thought he was real smart picking such an out-of-the-way trail – must have thought we were dumb.'

His brother Ernie showed a gap-toothed smile beneath his large moustache. 'I'll bet the sonofabitch hadn't figured on this rain. You only have to spit upstream in the San Tomas and it floods. We've got him now.'

'You might have him,' said Clem Mandle, the third member of the group. 'But if he digs in at the crossing he might be a bit hard to get at. He's reckoned to be pretty good with a gun.'

Ernie growled, 'If he was that good he wouldn't have needed that small army of gunslingers he used to have.'

Tony Santos was feeling so good that he even allowed himself another smile. 'He won't be any trouble at all to us. I figured he might run in this direction and I've hired Missouri Sam to watch for him. He's already at Red Rock Crossing. Grant won't know what hit him.'

Ernie and Mandle had never met Missouri Sam but knew of his reputation. He was a man who enjoyed killing; a shadowy figure who came and went and left corpses behind him. He was skilled at his work and so fearless that even hardened gunmen steered clear of him. It was claimed that Missouri operated in many guises and those who thought they would see a typical frontier gunman were disappointed when they first met him. But there was no doubting his results. Much was suspected against him but nothing had ever been proved. Missouri planned meticulously and carefully covered his tracks. Though plenty was whispered about him, little was said openly.

Tony Santos gathered up his reins and urged his mount forward. 'We can't sit here talking all day. We need to see Grant in Red Rock Crossing.'

'What's the hurry if Missouri Sam is waiting there for him already?' Mandle asked.

Ernie Santos told him. 'We want to fix that mangy sonofabitch ourselves. Missouri is just extra insurance to stop him getting away. He's been told to kill him only if he has to. It might come to that if Grant recognizes him Some of the big cattlemen used to hire him to run nesters off the range and Grant might have been one of them.'

'Sounds like you have things pretty well tied up,' Mandle observed. 'Fixing Grant should be easy.'

Tony growled, 'Don't get too cocky about it. Things always seem to go wrong when jobs look easy. I prefer to think some things will be hard and then be pleasantly surprised if they ain't. Now shake up those horses. We don't want to be hunting Grant in the dark.'

TWO

Ben and Marty paused long enough to greet Jane before riding to the stables behind the hotel to put up their horses. They felt it safer for all concerned if they camped in the stables with Hamel and got their meals from the hotel. Neither fancied keeping their prisoner overnight in a town with no proper jailhouse, but they had little option. One glance at the raging, brown water told them that any attempt at crossing would be suicidal.

They turned over their mounts to Pedro, the elderly Mexican groom who had worked for the Shelley family for most of his life, and arranged to secure their prisoner. Marty had a length of light, strong chain and two sturdy padlocks. He locked one end around the prisoner's ankle and the other around a solid post in the stable. 'Now, if you behave yourself, Eric, I'll take those cuffs off you so you're a bit more comfortable – but if you try to get away, I'll kill you. Is that plain enough?'

'I understand – I know you'd shoot me quick if I

gave you an excuse. I ain't crazy.'

'That's good to know. Any time you're off this chain you'll have the cuffs on and one of us will be with you at all times.' Marty turned to Ben. 'We'll take turn about watching Mr Hamel here. You go and see your girl. You're like someone standing on an ant hill. It's making me nervous just to watch you. I'll take first watch.'

Ben left the stable quickly in case his partner should suddenly change his mind.

Jane was waiting for him at the reception desk, but to his disappointment she was not alone. Jesse Grant was booking a room. With two Texas Rangers in town, he was feeling a bit more relaxed. He knew Ben by sight and when Jane introduced him, he asked, 'Did you see any other riders on the trail?'

'Not a one, but that don't mean there's none around. With a prisoner like Hamel, who has a lot of friends, my partner and I both suspect that we could have some of his men on our trail. Are you expecting trouble too?'

'The Santos brothers swore to get me,' Grant said. 'I came this way thinking I'd shake them off, but hadn't counted on the crossing being flooded. I'm mighty pleased to know there are a couple of rangers in town.'

Further conversation was cut short by the sound of gunshots coming from the saloon across the road.

Ben left in a hurry and ran to the stables where he found Marty looking anxiously towards the source of the noise. 'Stay here, Marty,' he ordered, 'and keep your eyes peeled. This might be a diversion caused by Hamel's friends.'

With shouted agreement from his partner, he drew his gun and sprinted across the muddy street to the long, low adobe building that was Dawson's saloon. Another shot rang out as he reached the door. A raucous burst of laughter followed it, then another shot.

The ranger peered around the doorpost and saw the dimly lit interior wreathed in gunsmoke. There was no mistaking Dawson, a powerfully built man in his late thirties who was beginning to run to fat. He had dark curly hair and a broad, brutal face adorned by a small goatee beard and moustache. He was looking quite pleased with himself as he stood behind the bar with a sawn-off shotgun pointing at a pale-faced man in town clothes who was cowering at the back of the room. Not far from his victim stood another man, also heavily built, a cowhand by his clothes. He had a smoking gun in his hand and the smile on his unshaven face was the same as the saloon owner's. A couple of the bar's other patrons were crouching anxiously behind overturned tables and each other.

'Rangers here,' Ben called. 'Put those guns down.'

The cowhand made no move to comply. He sneered, 'How do I know you're a ranger? You ain't wearin' a badge. You could be one of this four-flusher's friends. I ain't puttin' down my gun for you.'

20

Like most rangers, Ben did not weat his badge openly. Never taking his eyes from the man with the gun, he said, 'Dawson knows I'm a ranger – tell him Dawson.'

The saloon owner chuckled. He and Ben had clashed on several occasions and little love was lost between them. 'What if I don't? The light's pretty bad in here. If you was to get shot because you barged in here during a gunfight, no court would convict me. It would all be a big misunderstanding. Jasper here don't know you're a ranger. Anyway, he was just firing a few shots around this tinhorn's feet. There's no need for you to interfere. So don't bite off more than you can chew, Lawton. Now get out of this place, because I can cut you in half with this scattergun if you're looking for a fight.'

'You can try any time you like,' the ranger told him calmly. 'I'm not leaving without that man you were hassling, and if you attempt to cock a hammer on that cannon, I'll kill you.'

'Do you think you can?' Dawson challenged.

'I know I can, so put that gun down or use it.'

Suddenly a small figure came through the door, hands raised to show that he meant no harm. 'Now men,' Waldren said, 'what is so bad here that people need to be killed? Just stop and think a while. Killing is not a solution. It will only make matters worse.'

'Shut up, you psalm-singing little coyote,' the cowhand snarled. 'I can't stand you sanctimonious sonsofbitches, praying on your knees on Sundays and preying on everyone else for the rest of the week.'

'That goes for me too,' Dawson said. 'Now get out of here before you get shot.'

Ben reminded them, 'I have a partner here at the crossing and if anything happens me, or the reverend here, he'll hunt down those responsible. But he won't get you, Dawson, because I'll make sure I kill you even if you get me. If I as much as think that someone here is going to fire another shot, you're dead.'

The saloon owner swallowed hard and suddenly seemed lost for words. He knew that Ben was not bluffing. He looked towards Jasper, his eyes telling the bully to put away his gun.

Without taking his eyes off Dawson and the cowhand, the ranger said, 'Everyone who doesn't want to get involved in a shooting match had better walk out behind me. Just don't get between me and Dawson. Get moving.'

Cautiously the patrons left cover and filed out behind the ranger. The man in the town suit joined the exodus keeping a serape-clad Mexican between himself and his late tormentors.

'That mangy coyote's a card cheat,' Jasper protested, as he saw his victim leaving. 'He cheated me out of a three-dollar pot.'

'Surely you would not kill a man for three dollars,' Waldren said in a shocked tone.

'I'd kill that skunk for practice.'

With the innocent bystanders out of the way, Ben

said, quietly, 'The reverend and I are leaving now. If anything happens to that dude I'll come gunning for you, Dawson. I won't be leaving town for a while with the crossing the way it is.'

The saloon-keeper just glowered and Ben being able to walk out the door was living proof that looks, no matter how malevolent, did not kill.

Marty was hurrying towards the saloon, gun in hand when his partner emerged. 'I had to get Pedro to keep an eye on Hamel before I could come,' he explained. 'What happened?'

'Dawson and some drunken cowhand were giving a drummer a bad time. They didn't like me interfering and it looked serious for a while until the reverend walked in like he was at a church social and threw them off their game. I'm telling you, Marty, one of us will have to shoot Dawson one day, if he keeps going the way he is. He's half crazy – probably from drinking too much of his own whiskey.'

Jane was waiting on the hotel veranda, and her father stood beside her, a tall grey-haired man with plaster on his left foot, crutches under his arms and a big Remington revolver in one hand.

'Glad to see you ain't hurt, Ben. Jane was sure you were going to be killed. I wasn't fancying crossing all that mud on my crutches, let alone getting involved in a shooting match.'

'Thanks, Mr. Shelley, but I reckon the reverend over there stopped the situation getting too bad. When he finishes converting that drummer we just saved I must thank him.'

Jane's mother, Agnes, had obviously been interrupted while preparing meals and joined her husband and daughter with her sleeves rolled up and flour still on her hands. 'Be careful of Dawson, Ben,' she said in a worried tone. 'He's not very rational and has a short fuse and a long memory.'

The ranger assured her that he would and sought out the preacher. Waldren was standing at the end of the veranda in serious conversation with the still, pale-faced young man they had rescued. The drummer, seeing Ben, promptly took his leave of Waldren and hurried across to the ranger and thanked him. He said his name was Chester Rushton and that he was a footwear salesman. He had been coerced into the card game and had been winning honestly.

Ben told Rushton to be careful and stay clear of the saloon. Then he thanked the reverend for his assistance. But he warned, 'Don't push your luck too far, Reverend. Men like Dawson don't always listen to what you have to say and are likely to shoot first.'

A strange smile came to the little man's battered features. 'The Lord protected me all through the Civil War so He must have important work for me to do. If someone should interrupt that work, the vengeance of Heaven will fall upon them.'

Feeling a sermon coming on, Ben excused himself. He had volunteered to guard Hamel while Marty had a chance to look around town and socialize for a while.

Before the ranger left the hotel though, Joshua Shelley also made his contribution regarding the card game. It was a trick that was happening more and more in Dawson's saloon, he told the others. A visitor would be intimidated into joining a card game and would not be allowed to leave until all his money was gone. Anyone foolish enough to win would be beaten up and robbed anyway on the pretext that he had been cheating.

Shelley also enlightened the ranger about Waldren. He had appeared at the crossing a couple of days ago. The man had no religious training and did not claim to belong to any special denomination. He declared that he had been called to save sinners in the West and set out on his task with only his battered Bible, a skinny riding mule and a shotgun for hunting game along the way. The hotel keeper suggested that Waldren was not particularly well versed in the Bible and seemed to be learning as he went. He ventured the opinion that he had an old coon hound that would know as much about religion.

'That might be so,' Ben said, 'but he has a ton of guts. He walked into Dawson's place as though he was bullet-proof.'

'If he keeps hanging around Dawson's place, he'll need to be,' Shelley growled.

The light was fast fading when the three horsemen rode into Red Rock Crossing. They could hear the roaring of the flood above the sound of the rain and knew that Grant could not have crossed the river.

Their first stop was the livery stable. The owner had been about to close for the night when the trio rode up and dismounted. While arranging to stable their horses, they questioned the man about Grant.

'He's here. I saw him drive in. He's staying at Shelley's hotel. There's a couple of rangers and a prisoner there too,' the man said. 'They have a few stables for their guests' animals so he didn't come here.'

Tony Santos took a five-dollar note from his pocket. 'Feed those cayuses well and keep the change,' he said, 'and leave the stable door unlocked in case we have to leave town in a hurry. Where can we get a feed around here?'

'There's the hotel or a cheaper cantina next to Dawson's saloon.'

'The cantina sounds fine,' Santos told him. 'We don't want to walk too far in the rain.'

The three went out again into the downpour. They were cold and hungry and reckoned that a shot of whiskey would slip down nicely after a meal.

Across the road in his upstairs room, Grant was watching the street. He saw the three riders arrive and though he suspected the worst, he could not identify the men because of the poor light. It relieved him greatly to see that they did not cross the road but walked around the corner to the cantina near the saloon. As long as they stayed there he did not have to worry, but he dared not leave the window in case the newcomers returned unnoticed.

Downstairs, Jane and Ben were alone at last, sitting together on a long seat in the reception area and looking out the open doors of the hotel at the rain. After looking to be sure that nobody was about, the ranger slipped an arm around the girl's shoulder and held her close.

'It's nice sitting here with you and watching the rain,' he said. 'It sure beats sharing a stable with Marty and Hamel.'

'I should hope so,' Jane said, with pretended indignation.

'For purely selfish reasons, I don't mind the floods being over the crossing, but for safety's sake, the sooner we get over the San Tomas, the better.'

The girl looked concerned. 'Are you expecting some sort of trouble to catch up with you while you are here?'

'Nothing for sure but some of Hamel's boys might try to rescue him. And then there's that problem of Grant and the Santos brothers. While we are here we have to stop them killing each other and that's a responsibility that Marty and I had not counted on.'

'But the Santos brothers aren't here, are they?'

'I reckon they are,' Ben said slowly. 'Three riders rode in about half an hour ago. Marty thought he recognized Tony Santos. They might come here later looking for rooms. If you don't want your hotel full of bullet holes, it might be safer to say you have no vacancies.'

Any further conversation was interrupted by the sound of boots on the boardwalk outside. The couple moved apart, their eyes fixed on the open door but nobody entered. As though deep in thought, Waldren walked past the doorway without even glancing in.

'I wonder what he's up to,' Ben said. 'Looks like he's headed for the saloon. Maybe he's about to come off the wagon.'

'Not a chance,' Jane laughed. 'He's probably waiting to discourage anyone from going into Dawson's saloon. He does not approve of alcohol in any form.'

'Is he staying at the hotel?'

'No. He's camping in a derelict building that used to be an old shop. This town's gradually dying and that river you can hear out there is the main problem. In wet weather it delays too many travellers, so most folks avoid travelling by this crossing now.'

Ten miles south of Red Rock Crossing, Gus Martin found the cave he had been seeking. It was large and dry and had a rocky overhang that would protect the horses when they were tethered. Martin's outlaw career had taken him all over the South-West and he knew scores of places where there was shelter away from the prying eyes of more honest people. He was a hard-faced man of medium size, somewhere in his late thirties, a man who wore a pair of guns and needed little urging to use them. He was dressed in the rough clothing of a frontiersman and had it not been for the two guns, he would not have been noticed among the ordinary townspeople.

Joe Owens, the only other survivor of the Hamel gang, looked young and innocent when compared to his older partner except for his cold, narrow blue eyes, the eyes of a killer. Owens wore only one gun openly, but had various other weapons hidden about his person. He was good with them all.

'There's no need to hurry now,' Martin said, as he pulled the saddle off his horse. 'The San Tomas will surely be up by now and those rangers will have to cool their heels at the crossing at least for another two days. They won't be expecting to have us on their backs.'

Owens placed his saddle in a sheltered spot before asking, 'Don't you reckon them rangers will be expecting us to try something?'

'It won't help them if they are. We won't go barging in there looking for trouble. If we do our job right, they'll be dead before they know we're around.'

THREE

Tony Santos met Missouri Sam in the most unexpected place, the outhouse behind Dawson's saloon. He would not have recognized him as he had been posing as a rich cattle buyer at their last meeting, but an agreed-upon recognition signal confirmed that he had the right man. After a brief whispered conversation, he returned to his brother and Mandle.

'I've just been talking to Missouri. He reckons there's a couple of rangers in town. If anything happens to Grant while we are still here, they'll be looking for us. I told him that we'd stay where plenty of witnesses were about and leave the job to him.'

Ernie Santos looked doubtful. 'We'll still be blamed for killing Grant. Everyone knows he had our pa murdered.'

'Grant was never charged with Pa's murder because he paid someone else to do it,' Tony said bitterly. 'Two can play that game.'

'Sort of poetic justice,' Mandle suggested. 'I've

never seen this Missouri *hombre*. What does he look like?'

'You're better not knowing. I wouldn't have known him tonight. He's a creepy sonofabitch. Reminds me of a rattlesnake except he don't give no warnings. He just enjoys killing people; I think he's going a little crazy. Too bad he can't take Grant somewhere quiet and kill him real slow. I know he'd enjoy it.'

'What happens now?' Mandle asked.

Tony pulled a roll of bills from his pocket. 'I'll pay Dawson to keep the place open and I'll buy a few drinks for the bar. It's important that folks remember right where we are tonight.'

From the derelict building where he had been staying, Missouri heard the sounds of drunken revelry and knew that Santos was making sure that people remembered where he was. Some might have wished themselves part of the celebrations – but not Missouri. He enjoyed killing and was actually looking forward to the task ahead, Carefully he assembled his tools for the job. He attached a holster to his belt. It contained a Navy Colt that had been shortened and converted to take .38 centre-fire cartridges. A sheath knife on the other side of the belt partially balanced the gun. The knife was a crude-looking affair with a five-inch blade made from an old saw and had a rough wooden handle, but the blade had been honed to razor-sharpness. He also looped a short length of strong cord under his belt where he could grab it quickly. On a couple of occasions he had found it necessary to strangle his victims. Finally, he replaced his hat with a black hood with eyeholes and exchanged his boots for moccasins. In his dark clothing and soft footwear it was unlikely that he would be seen or heard.

He had studied the layout of the hotel. The Shelley family lived in part of the upper floor and the rest was taken up with guest rooms and a bathroom. Red Rock Crossing was slowly dying and Missouri knew that there were few guests. He assumed that Grant would want a room that overlooked the street. Entry by the window was out of the question and he knew that the best way to get at his victim would be through the door that opened into the hallway. He knew that the doors of most western hotels were fairly flimsy with cheap, easily opened locks. One good kick would open it. He had seen Shelley on crutches and knew that if all else failed, he could kick open the door and shoot Grant before the hotel keeper could intervene. But the killer preferred a more silent approach. When someone was found murdered and nobody had seen or heard anything suspicious, it added to the impact of the killing.

The rain had been stopped for an hour when Missouri eased himself quietly out the sagging door of the derelict building and silently made his way to the hotel. He was prepared to break in if necessary but found the double doors on the front entrance, though closed against the weather, were unlocked. Through the glass he could see that the front desk was unattended. The doors opened silently and the killer slipped through before closing them quietly behind him again. He crouched for a moment keeping below the level of the reception desk as he took stock of his surroundings.

A light showed in the nearby office window. Jane was sitting up late in the small private office behind the ground-floor reception desk. The rest of the family and customers had all retired but she had been catching up on some overdue office work. She had been there an hour and the monotony of the accounts and the continuous roar of the flooded river had finally taken their toll. Yawning and sleepy, she stood up and began to put away the account books.

Missouri heard her moving about as he kept below the level of the reception desk while planning his next move. Most of the lamps were out. There was only the one in the office and one on the stairs for the guidance of late-returning guests, so much of the area was in deep shadows. Silently he crept to a dark space at the end of a large sofa and crouched there. He would have to wait until the girl went upstairs. It would not do to have a witness between him and his escape route after he had killed Grant.

Jane tidied the office and went to lock the front doors for the night. As she bent to secure the lower bolts she saw fresh mud on the floor. There was more of it in front of the reception desk and a trail led across the floor to a gloomy corner near the sofa..

Her eyes followed it and, to her horror, she saw a vague shape in the shadows. Something showed above the end of the sofa, a dark misshapen thing like the head of some monstrous being. She sensed rather than knew that it was a man. Terror jolted through her. She had to flee, but in which direction? The menacing intruder was between her and the stairs. Fleeing outside was not an option as there would be no time to unbolt the front doors.

Missouri heard the sharp intake of breath and saw the fear on Jane's face. She had seen him, and in seconds would scream. He had to silence her quickly. He bounded from concealment in an effort to reach her before she could call for help. He dragged the length of cord from his belt as he came.

But if the killer was expecting a fear-frozen victim, he was mistaken. Jane moved with unexpected speed, dodged around the end of the desk, threw herself through the office door and slammed it, letting out a piercing scream as she did so. The killer was just a fraction of a second too slow. The door shook as Missouri hurled himself against it.

There was a loaded gun in a desk drawer in the office but the girl knew that she had to hold the door shut and could not reach it. She screamed again. Loud and piercing, the sound echoed through the silent hotel.

The door shook as Missouri hit it again in blind rage. Nobody had ever escaped him before. He drew his knife and plunged it into the thin wooden panelling. The tip of the blade missed the girl by inches and she screamed louder than ever.

Then the instinct for survival brought Missouri's homicidal madness under control. Footsteps and doors banging in upstairs rooms told him that he would have to flee.

He heard Shelley anxiously calling his daughter and heard the dull thump of crutches on the stairs. In seconds, he had sprinted from the office to the front door and jerked open the bolts that secured it. A gun blasted behind him as Shelley snapped a shot at the dark figure in the open doorway. The bullet missed but broke a glass panel while Missouri fled into the night.

'Jane! Are you all right?'

To her father's intense relief, his daughter opened the office door. She was pale and trembling but unharmed. She was also clutching a small revolver in her hand.

As her relieved father wrapped a comforting arm around her, the girl said in a shaky voice, 'He was hiding in the shadows – I think he was trying to kill me.'

At this point, boots clattered on the boardwalk outside, and Ben rushed in with his Colt drawn. He had heard the scream and the shot and came running. 'What's happening?' he demanded.

A brief explanation followed and the ranger set out after the intruder. A trail of muddy footprints indicated the direction in which the man had bolted.

They stopped where the boardwalk ended at the mouth of an alley. Ben was about to enter the alley when he discerned a moving figure further down the road in front of one of the derelict buildings. 'Stay where you are,' he called as he cocked his gun.

Waldren's voice came back. 'Be careful, my friend. It is only me. I heard the noise and thought I might be needed. Is the lady all right?'

'Come forward quietly and keep your hands where I can see them.'

The preacher walked forward slowly. He was hatless and coatless and his hair was dishevelled. He kept both hands well away from his sides. 'What's happening, Ben?'

'What are you doing out at this time of night, Reverend?'

'Until a short while ago, I was sleeping. A scream woke me and then I heard a shot. I just jumped into my boots and was coming to see if I could help.'

'Did you hear anyone run past?'

The preacher shook his head. 'I can't say that I did but I'm a bit hard of hearing and the river roaring like it is does not help.'

The preacher's boots were muddy but it was not fresh mud. Ben had a look around but there were several derelict buildings and a few stranded travellers were camped in them. The ranger went from one ruin to another but found nothing significant. The majority of the campers had been awakened by the gunshot but a couple snored through it all. None had seen anything unusual. Gradually his anger cooled and, realizing that he was wasting his time, the ranger returned to the hotel. He paused at the door when he saw the Santos brothers and Mandle just leaving the saloon. They were obviously drunk and seemed more interested in finding their way to bed than they were in the ranger regarding them suspiciously from across the road. They would spend the night in a small adobe building behind the saloon that Dawson also owned and allowed certain of his better customers to use. After the money they had spent during the evening, Santos and his companions had earned promotion into that category.

Ben could only report failure in his search for the intruder. While he was away, Shelley had sent Pedro to appraise Marty of the situation as the other ranger could not leave his prisoner. Jane was still pale and shaken but could give little information about the attacker. They were standing in a group discussing the intruder's motives when Grant joined them. In a tired voice, he told them, 'I think you'll find he was after me.'

FOUR

Ernie Santos heard the news first. He relayed it to Tony who, with a violent hangover, was just struggling clear of his blankets. 'Missouri missed Grant last night,' he said. 'All he did was scare the Shelley girl at the hotel. Looks like we might have to fix that *hombre* ourselves.'

'Like hell we will,' his brother declared, and shuddered at the effect of his own voice on his headache. 'Missouri cost us plenty and I want my money's worth. That river will stay high for at least another day so he can try again some other time.'

Mandle joined them then. He had been outside being violently ill. 'That whiskey of Dawson's goes down fine,' he gasped, 'but it has fish hooks in it when it comes up next morning. I just heard talk about someone getting into the hotel last night. One of them rangers chased him but lost him in some of them empty houses down the road.'

'Did anyone see who it was?' Tony croaked.

'Only the hotel girl that he scared, but she didn't

38

get much of a look at him. The feller that told me reckoned he was wearing a mask.'

'Our luck's still holding,' Ernie told them.

'I wish my guts were,' Mandle moaned, and lurched out of the door again.

After finishing his shift of guard duty, Ben sought out Jane. He found her in the hotel reception area. She had recovered from the previous night's experience and announced her intention of never being caught at such a disadvantage again. She had placed the revolver in a more convenient drawer of the reception desk.

'If our friend comes back tonight, he's in for a shock,' she announced. The tone of the girl's voice showed that she would take a more active role in her own defence if a similar situation ever arose again. She was more angry than frightened.

'You still have no idea of who he was, or what he was after?' Ben asked.

'He was wearing some sort of mask. Mr. Grant thinks he was after him but he could have been just a thief or a madman. If I had not seen the fresh mud on the floor, I would not have known he was there. I don't think I have ever been so frightened.'

'But you kept your head,' the ranger told her. 'You're some girl, Jane Shelley. My problem now is to find whoever it was before I have to leave. That river will start dropping soon and Marty and I have to be on our way then. We don't want any of Hamel's men trying to rescue him.'

Over the road in Dawson's saloon, Tony Santos told the others, 'We might have to make these our last drinks. I'm thinking it's nearly time we were gone.'

'But we ain't fixed Grant yet; Missouri missed him last night,' his brother growled.

'Don't worry. I saw him a while ago at the livery stable when I was checking on our horses. He reckons that Grant won't get over the river alive.'

'I'd still like to see what Missouri looks like,' Ernie grumbled.

The older Santos brother explained. 'Missouri reckons it safest for all concerned that you don't know what he looks like. Just leave things the way they are. That way folks can't tie you to Missouri if things go wrong.'

Ernie was not convinced about Grant's impending demise and reminded his brother that the assassin had failed before. He argued that they should see the job done before they left Red Rock Crossing. Mandle was of a similar opinion, although his main purpose was to stay closer to the whiskey supply. Eventually Tony gave in figuring that another day in the saloon would not matter. They would be back to ranch work soon enough. He reminded the others though that they were to stay around witnesses all the time until the deed was known to be done.

Ben, after he left Jane, started checking the derelict buildings again. Relics of the days when Red

Rock Crossing had a larger population, most were without doors or windows. Some had even had the floorboards torn up for firewood. Tramps and travellers who could not afford hotel rooms had been camped in some of those buildings sharing them with rats and the occasional snake. Ben was very conscious of the latter as he picked his way over broken floorboards. Floods had always flushed out numerous snakes and the derelict buildings provided them with a refuge. Few people would camp in these ruins by choice, but in wet weather any sort of a roof looked good to those who could not afford better shelter.

He found Waldren living in one ruin but excused himself quickly in case he was subjected to another sermon. Next door he met a Mexican who was just leaving. He was a wiry little man of uncertain age with a short beard and an old single-barrel shotgun held by the muzzle, slung over his shoulder. He announced that he was going along the river-bank to see if he could get a rabbit for his evening meal. In response to the ranger's questioning, he said that his name was Emilio Gonzales and he was making his way north in the hope of picking up ranch work. He denied seeing or hearing anything suspicious during the previous night, although he had heard the shot that Shelley had fired.

The next ruined house was sheltering acouple of men, Virgil Brown and his son, Neither was happy to see the ranger. The pair had been taking a load of illegally distilled whiskey to Three Mesas when the flooded river stopped them. Neither was at ease being questioned by a ranger and gave guarded answers. But Ben was interested in more important criminals and did not ask embarrassing questions about the reason for their travels. Like Gonzales and the others, the Browns could add little to what the lawman already knew. When he returned to relieve Marty, he was still none the wiser as to the identity or the true motives of the mysterious attacker.

FIVE

Missouri was reconnoitring the town when his luck changed for the better. He was standing by the riverbank when he looked back at the hotel and saw Grant looking out of a second-storey window. Suddenly his problems were solved. He knew where his target was. He also knew that a man who had virtually imprisoned himself in a room, could not stay away from the window. While thinking himself safe, Grant had actually made himself a target.

Missouri quickly found the place he was seeking. It was the tallest cottonwood in a clump on the riverbank. The foliage of other trees growing nearby would help conceal the shooter from people at street level. The tree was easy to climb for someone as agile as the killer and it gave a good view of Grant's hotel window about eighty yards away. Now it was just a matter of waiting.

Few people were moving around the town but Missouri needed the right circumstances for his plan to work. He could not reduce the sound of the shot, but if nobody was on the street, people would be unsure of where it had originated. He knew that Grant was keeping to his room but was fully aware that boredom would have him looking out his window. At some time that afternoon, the street would be empty and Grant would be looking out the window. Missouri would be waiting.

Hamel, in his makeshift confinement behind the hotel, was starting to get restless. 'Are you sure that water's still high?' he demanded of Ben, as he tugged impatiently at the chain around his ankle.

'Take it easy, Eric. At least we're getting well fed while we're stuck here. If I was in your boots, I would-n't be in any hurry to go where Marty and I are taking you. Relax and enjoy the easy times while you can.'

The prisoner could not be bothered replying. He was sure that the survivors of his gang would be somewhere on his trail and that their intentions were unlikely to be friendly. It had seemed a good plan to escape with a bank's takings and leave his henchmen shooting things out with angry townsfolk. He had not counted on Martin and Owens fighting their way clear of the trap. Any reunion between himself and the survivors would not be a happy one. They wanted their share of the loot and were sure to be seeking to avenge his desertion of them.

'I would have thought that your friends might try to free you,' Ben told Hamel. 'Being delayed here would suit you more than it suits me.'

The prisoner made no comment but secretly

44

preferred years in prison to the fate he knew awaited him if he fell into the clutches of his former friends.

'Would you like me to get that preacher fellow, Waldren, to have a few words with you?' the ranger teased. 'You must be sick of the look of Marty and me.'

Hamel was not amused. 'Keep that psalm-singing coyote away from me. I don't believe in all that stuff.'

Marty arrived then. He had been taking a break from guard duty and walking around town looking for any signs of trouble. 'The river's still up,' he announced. 'There must have been heavy rain upstream. We won't be getting out today.'

'No sign of trouble?'

Marty chuckled. 'I saw Waldren, that preacher fellow, down by the river so I slipped away quietly before he saw me. I didn't feel much like a sermon today.'

'That's one thing you and Hamel have in common: he don't feel like a visit from the preacher today either.'

'Go to hell, the pair of you,' the prisoner snarled.

Jesse Grant was a puzzled man. The Santos brothers were in town. He knew that. They had sworn to kill him, but to all intents and purposes were deliberately staying away from where he was. He was certain that the intruder the night before had been after him although others were not so sure. As much as possible, he stayed in his room and, understanding his circumstances, the Shelleys were happy to bring his meals to him. He had been lucky that the rangers had arrived when they did and intended to attach himself to them for protection when the river eventually dropped and he could start travelling again. But they could not make him bullet-proof, or protect him from a long-range rifle shot.

Utter boredom was setting in and more and more Grant found himself looking out the window. Very little was happening in the street, but he could see across it to the river. At places some ancient cottonwoods obscured the view but he could see a fair stretch of the stream, enough to show that it was still too high to cross. The self-imprisoned man was beginning to find something comforting about standing at the window, smoking his pipe and watching the flood swirl past. In a less worrying time, the roar of the water would have had a soothing effect.

'I've changed my mind; I'm sick of this town. I don't think my liver will take any more of Dawson's rotgut,' Ernie Santos complained to his brother. 'Let's go home and leave the job to Missouri.'

'It's because Missouri is doing the job that we have to stay here. Right out in the open so everyone can see that it wasn't us that settled Grant's hash,' Tony growled.

Mandle agreed with him. 'Tony's right, Ernie. You'll know when the job's been done and nobody can point the finger at you. Just cool your heels for a while.'

Half-drunk and angry, Ernie pushed back his chair, stood up and glared around the saloon. He was a fighting drunk but was rather selective of his opponents. They had to be weaker, smaller and preferably drunker. He lurched out into the street looking for a victim and promptly found one.

Chester Rushton had avoided Dawson's saloon since his first experience there and was sitting on a seat on the hotel veranda reading a newspaper. He was not drunk, but being small and of slight build and wearing city clothes, the young man attracted Ernie Santos like a lamb would attract a wolf.

Some inbuilt instinct seemed to warn the drummer of approaching trouble. He put down his newspaper – but too late.

'You,' Santos bellowed. He had seen Rushton about to retreat into the hotel. 'Stay right where you are.' To add weight to his order, the brawler drew his gun.

Rushton froze.

'Stay right where you are, or I'll kill you, fancy pants.'

Ben was talking to Jane in the hotel office when he heard the shouting. 'There's trouble outside,' he said. 'Stay here.' In the long-established ranger tradition, he drew his gun as he went. He could always return it to his holster if it was not needed, but men who walked into trouble with their guns in their holsters did not last long.

The ranger walked out onto the veranda in time to see Santos waving his cocked gun in Rushton's direction. The young man had gone pale knowing that the weapon might discharge accidentally at any time. Further down the street, he saw that the drinkers from Dawson's place had emerged to watch what they considered to be fun.

'I'm a Texas Ranger,' Ben called. 'Put that gun away.'

Santos did not hesitate. He switched his aim to the newcomer and fired. In his current mood, nobody told Ernie Santos what to do. The shot went through the front wall of the hotel.

Ben fired then. His bullet clipped Santos's hip and spun him sideways causing the wounded man to fire an involuntary shot as he struggled to stay on his feet.

'Drop your gun!' Ben called urgently.

Shocked into sobriety, Santos might have obeyed if Mandle had not decided to take a hand in the proceedings. He fired a long-range shot that tore a long splinter from the veranda rail beside the ranger. It was the last shot he ever fired.

Marty came around the corner, took in the scene and fired his Winchester from the hip. The bullet took Mandle under the arm and drove him violently sideways as it smashed him to the ground. He struggled to rise, made a choking sound and fell back dead.

Tony Santos who was about to join in the fighting, had second thoughts and raised his hands on Marty's command. His brother had fired again for no result and Ben's return shot tore along his right arm. The gun flew from his hand. The shots were still echoing around the hills when Ernie Santos flopped into a sitting position on the ground.

Jane burst out the front door with an angry look on her face and a small revolver in her hand. Close behind her, Josh Shelley came out on his crutches also holding a revolver.

'Get back inside, Jane,' Ben ordered.

'It's safer out here,' the girl said angrily. 'A bullet just missed me. It came through the office wall. If those drunken no-goods want a fight, they can have it.'

But the fight had gone out of the others. Covered by Marty's Winchester on one side and confronted by Ben on the other, none of them dared try his luck in such a high-stakes game.

Cautiously, Ben approached the wounded gunman who was alternately gasping in pain and snarling at the man who had caused it. He picked up the fallen gun and called to Marty, 'How's the other one?'

Keeping his eyes on the group before him, the other ranger called back, 'This one's dead.' Then he turned to Tony Santos. 'You'd better see if you can help your brother – but don't try anything stupid.'

Mumbling curses under his breath, Tony hurried to his brother's side but he kept his hands well clear of his gun.

Missouri saw it all from his perch in the cotton-wood tree. He felt very pleased with himself. At first he had cursed Ernie Santos for bringing people onto the street but the shooting gave him the opportunity he had been seeking.

Curiosity had proved Jesse Grant's undoing. When he came to his open window to see what was happening, he walked straight into Missouri's sights, A gentle squeeze of the trigger and the waiting killer sent a .44/40 bullet into the centre of his target's chest. Amid the echoes of the other shots, Missouri heard the thump of the bullet striking home. His victim disappeared from view, but the shooter had no doubt that he had scored a killing shot. He had practised with his weapon regularly and at the range involved knew that he would not miss. After ejecting the empty shell, he climbed down from the tree. It was time to be seen again.

In front of the hotel, chaos reigned. The wounded man was cursing as his brother hurried to his aid. Dawson and the hangers-on from the saloon were loudly proclaiming that Marty had murdered Mandle and the two rangers were trying to restore some semblance of order.

Ben was worried too about leaving their prisoner unguarded. His partner assured him that he was temporarily secure as he had been left handcuffed around a stable post. Marty had guessed when he heard the raised voices that Ben could be in trouble and was forced to leave their prisoner to protect his comrade.

'Dawson's crowd are claiming that I murdered that man,' Marty protested to Josh Shelley.

'Don't worry about it,' the hotel-keeper told him. 'There's enough of us here that are sober and we all saw what happened. That man tried to kill Ben and got what he deserved. We'll back you in court if it should come to that. One of their stray shots nearly hit Jane. It came straight through the office wall.'

'I'll try to get things settled down here,' Ben told his partner. 'It might be an idea if you got back to Hamel. He has more tricks than a barrel of monkeys.'

Suddenly the shabby figure of Waldren joined the group around the injured man. With arms raised as if in distress, he addressed the crowd. 'Please, brothers, let us have no more violence. See the misery it causes.'

'Shut up,' a voice came from the crowd.

The preacher continued, 'I will not be silent. This is wrong. We should not be spreading violence and hatred. Has anyone stopped cussing long enough to even say a prayer for that poor soul who was killed?'

Dawson chuckled. 'That wasn't any poor soul: that was Clem Mandle, one of the lowest back-shooters around these parts. The Devil's welcome to him.'

Waldren pointed his finger at Dawson. 'There's no doubt that the Devil's brew that you dispense had some part in this terrible tragedy. One day the Lord

51

will strike you, Dawson, just like Moses smote the Corinthians – or whoever they were.'

The latter comment brought a few chuckles from those who had a fleeting acquaintance with the Bible.

'Moses didn't smote no Corinthians.' shouted a bystander. 'He smote Goliath.'

'That was David,' a half-drunk cowhand corrected.

'It don't really matter if Moses smote David,' Waldren said earnestly, 'You know what I'm trying to say. All this killing and violence must stop.'

Dawson was starting to enjoy himself. 'But it will stop, Preacher, just as soon as every sonofabitch with a grudge kills everyone he don't like. The sooner they all kill each other, the sooner the rest of us can have a quiet life.'

Waldren threw up his hands in despair and walked away.

Josh Shelley nudged Ben. 'Like I said before, my old coon hound knows more about religion than that preacher does.'

Red Rock Crossing had no doctor and the raging San Tomas River was between the wounded Ernie Santos and the closest medical aid. Dawson's assistant barman had seen more than his share of bullet wounds, first as a hospital steward in the Civil War and more recently in his current work. He was able to dress the wounds and staunch the bleeding. There was a doctor at Turkey Springs forty miles to the south so Tony Santos arranged to borrow a buckboard from Dawson and hire a driver to take his brother there. He would remain at Red Rock Crossing and arrange the burial of Mandle. He cared little for the dead man, but he now had a good excuse to remain in town. As well as waiting to hear from Missouri, he now had a score to settle with the two rangers. Nobody shot a Santos or one of their men and lived to brag about it.

SIX

Hamel had plenty of time on his hands. With his ankle chain fastened to a strong post he was going nowhere. Consequently he had little to do but study his surroundings. It was only when the light fell a certain way through the stable window that he noticed the short length of thin wire lying under the edge of the straw upon which he was resting. The wire was within reach but with Marty a few yards away at the stable entrance, he did not wish to attract attention by openly moving toward it.

The ranger was reading a week-old newspaper and looked up when he heard the prisoner stirring.

Hamel began stretching out his limbs as if he was getting cramped. 'The sooner that river gets down, the better,' he complained. 'I'm sick of this flea-bitten town.'

Marty looked up from his newspaper. 'For once I agree with you, Hamel. I can see why horses get bored spending too much time in the stable.'

The prisoner squirmed around a little more as if

getting comfortable, but as soon as the ranger was concentrating on the paper again, he picked up the wire. Turning his back as though attempting to sleep, Hamel surreptitiously straightened the wire and doubled it. It was fine-gauge metal and he hoped that it would fit into the keyhole in the padlock. Experience had taught him that some outwardly solid locks had very weak locking mechanisms inside. He tossed and turned as though seeking a more comfortable position and finally curled himself into a ball so that his hand was close to his ankle. Working by feel, he inserted the wire in the keyhole and twisted it only to feel it bend in his hand. When he sought to withdraw it the wire stuck and, as he struggled to pull it free, the hasp of the lock moved.

Hamel was pleasantly surprised, as he had expected a long period of trying for doubtful results. He could quickly rid himself of the chain but now needed a weapon to tackle his younger, fitter and better-armed guard. He looked around and found one. A wooden box attached to a nearby stall contained a few lumps of well-licked rock salt for the horses. One piece was slightly larger than his fist and would do as an improvised club if he moved quickly enough. He knew that boredom made all guards careless, so pretended to sleep, but his mind was racing as he planned his escape.

Agnes Shelley, with a bundle of clean towels under one arm, knocked at the door of Grant's room. 'Mr

Grant,' she called, 'I have some clean towels for you.'

Silence.

She tried again. 'Mr Grant, I have some clean towels for you.' She half expected to hear a bed creak as the guest awoke from a nap but a few seconds later there was still no sound from the room. Surprised that the man had left his room unnoticed, she used her master key to open the door.

Agnes Shelley's scream was heard all over Red Rock Crossing.

Ben was talking to Jane when he heard the scream. He left the room and drew his gun as he bounded up the stairs three at a time. He turned into the corridor in time to see Agnes leaning weakly against a wall in the corridor. She was deathly pale and upon seeing the ranger, pointed to the open door beside her. 'It's Grant,' she half whispered. 'He's dead.'

Upon entering the room, Ben saw the former rancher lying flat on his back with a shocked look on his face and sightless eyes. The front of his shirt was soaked in blood and there was more on the rug beneath him. It only took a second to see that he had been shot while standing at the open window.

Jane arrived then and started attending to her shocked mother. Josh Shelley and Rushton arrived a short time later. The older man was cursing his crutches as he entered the room. 'What's happened?' he demanded.

'Someone killed Grant,' Ben replied. 'Looks like they shot him through the open window.'

'But I didn't hear a shot,' Shelley said.

'It was probably while Marty and I were swapping lead with Santos and his friend. Folks were too busy ducking for cover to be counting shots and they were echoing off the hills anyway.' The ranger walked to the window and studied the scene. 'The shooter must have been in those trees on the river-bank, just waiting for a chance.'

Shelley looked at the dead man and shook his head. 'Who would want to kill a man in cold blood like this?'

'The Santos brothers wanted to kill him but we all know that they didn't.' Ben turned to Rushton. 'Will you give the folks a hand here? I'll have to tell Marty what happened and I want to have a look over in those trees.'

Rushton agreed to help with the dead man and the ranger hurried to the stable to tell his partner of the latest development. Then he made his way to the river-bank.

Because of its proximity to the town, people who had been checking the river height had left many footprints along the bank. Ben could easily figure out the shooter's location because there was only one place that looked directly into Grant's window. He quickly found what he sought, a shiny brass cartridge case, a Winchester .44/40. It did not tell him anything new because such rifles were popular on the frontier and he would find many if he was to check every rifle in Red Rock Crossing.

Seated on a bale of hay with his back against a post and terribly bored, Marty found himself dozing. A couple of times he awoke with a start after nodding off. He looked around. Hamel was still stretched out on the straw with his eyes closed as though sleeping. Hurry up, Ben, he said to himself They would be changing duties shortly.

Hamel quietly slid the open hasp out of the chain and came to his feet as silently as a big cat. Reaching into the shallow wooden trough, he carefully lifted the largest lump of rock salt from it and with this clenched in his fist, advanced on the unsuspecting ranger.

Marty dozed for a second then awoke and shook his head. Expecting no real trouble he glanced over his shoulder. Too late.

Hamel swung his weighted fist, smashing the rock salt down on the ranger's head. The blow landed solidly and knocked the startled guard to the ground but his hat and a heavy leather hat band cushioned the blow. Badly dazed, Marty reached for his gun but his reactions were too slow. His hat had been dislodged and now there was nothing between his head and the descending blow. The lump of salt shattered upon impact in Hamel's hand but it had done its work and the ranger collapsed unconscious with blood pouring from his torn scalp. In seconds, the attacker had unbuckled Marty's gunbelt. As he ran, he buckled it around his own waist.

The horses were in the corral so he snatched up a bridle before fleeing from the stable. There would be no time to worry about a saddle. His hand was on the gate latch when he heard the command.

'Stop, Hamel!'

Ben had returned in time to see his partner bleeding on the ground and their prisoner about to enter the corral.

The distance between them was a long shot for a revolver so Hamel took a chance. With no prospects of getting a horse, he turned and ran away from the hotel, fleeing between the backs of the houses and the sharply rising bluff behind.

Ben fired but missed. Before he could shoot again, the outlaw had vanished into the brush growing on the hillside. The ranger did not pursue. He could see Marty moving slightly and his first priority was to gauge the extent of his injuries.

The injured man moved and groaned when he heard his partner's voice, but was totally disoriented when he opened his eyes.

'Marty – it's me, Ben. Are you OK?'

'What happened?'

'Hamel got loose and I have to get after him. Can you sit up?'

'Oh . . . my head. . . . What happened?'

'Hamel's loose. He hit you with something.'

Marty struggled to a sitting position but looked

blankly at his partner. The hand he put to his aching head came away covered in blood. He stared at it but had difficulty comprehending what had happened. Ben knew that he was severely concussed at best and might even have a fractured skull. The injured ranger had no recollection of how he had received his injuries.

At this point Pedro arrived.

'Look after him, Pedro,' Ben ordered. 'I have to get Hamel back.' Drawing his six-gun, the ranger started after the escaped prisoner.

The delay in pursuit that Marty's injury caused allowed the outlaw to gain a good start. About 200 yards past the houses, the San Tomas River ran into a sheer walled gorge. Hamel knew the area and was aware of a narrow path between the water's edge and the canyon wall. Once there and protected by irregularities in the rocks and the winding path, it would be easy to ambush anyone who was following. One ranger was out of the way and the outlaw knew that if he could dispose of the second, he could return to the town and help himself to a horse.

He was close to the entrance of the canyon when he realized that he had made a potentially fatal mistake. The canyon path was under water and he could not use it to escape. He would have to retrace his steps and somehow get past the ranger who would already be on his trail. The ground on his left as he looked back, sloped sharply, its brush-covered slopes eventually giving way to sheer rock walls.

Turning right was not an option as the town and the river were on that side. He had to go back and somehow ambush the ranger and kill him.

SEVEN

At first the path of Hamel's flight showed clearly with boot prints on bare earth and plenty of broken twigs as he fled through the chaparral on the hillside. In places it was possible to see where he had fallen on ground still slippery from the recent rain, but of the fugitive himself there was no sign. He had gone to ground somewhere in the low scrub.

Though unfamiliar with the area, Ben could see that the valley tapered down into a narrow gorge with sheer sides. Hamel could only escape by turning back on his tracks. It was then that he remembered his carbine: he had left it on his saddle in the stable. The task of covering the slope suddenly became much harder. Working on the assumption that the fugitive could see him, Ben dropped to the ground and kept below the level of the chaparral. He saw no point in letting his enemy know exactly where he was. Then he carefully changed position to a hiding place midway between the top and bottom of the slope and settled down to wait.

Hamel was already down in the chaparral and cursing his luck. Time was against him. If he remained too long where he was the other ranger might recover enough to come to Ben's aid, or even some of the town's citizens might join the hunt. He had a $500 reward on his head.

Ben crouched low and listened. He was not going anywhere. It was almost impossible for a man to move noiselessly through the chaparral. If he remained alert he would hear anyone approaching and need not show himself. He cocked his revolver so the sound would not betray him later when Hamel was in earshot.

Patience was one of the many virtues that were omitted from the outlaw's make-up. The reckless side of his nature was telling him to stand up and start shooting when Ben showed himself but he resisted the urge. As a bandit he rarely became engaged in stand-up gunfights and strongly suspected that the ranger might have had more practice in that area. Much as he hated the idea, Hamel would have to stalk and kill his man. The killing did not worry him but he had never been a great one for stealth. Flat on the ground, the outlaw began crawling through the low brush.

The soil was muddy and soon his clothing was stained and wet but his discomfort made Hamel all the more determined to kill his former captor.

Ben kept low trying to see under the chaparral and listening for the slightest sound. A mild breeze was blowing causing a gentle rustling in the leaves and silently the ranger cursed it because it could cover the sound of a stealthy approach. He knew that the fugitive had to come back past him. Would he go higher or lower on the slope, or was he creeping straight at him?

The minutes dragged by and doubts moved into Ben's mind. He was beginning to fear that somehow Hamel had already crept past him. He did not know how long he had been there. It could have been one minute or ten.

The outlaw had decided to move along the lower slope of the hill because the brush there was slightly higher and gave better concealment. Don't rush, he told himself. Let him make the first mistake.

Martin saw the onlookers as he and Owens came over the crest of the hill behind Red Rock Crossing. 'Looks like something's happening. Them *hombres* are watching something down behind the houses.'

His baby-faced companion did not like what he saw. He asked, 'How are we going to get Hamel away from them rangers with all those people looking on? It don't pay to have too many witnesses around. If they decide to take a hand we wouldn't have a chance.'

'Let's see what's happening,' Martin suggested. 'Looks like most of those fellers are from Dawson's saloon. Some have still got glasses in their hands. Chances are that if we don't throw any lead their way,

64

they won't interfere with us.'

The pair rode closer.

The first man they met was a wagon driver stopped by the flood. By his appearance, he had spent his enforced idleness mostly in the saloon. 'I'd get down off those horses if I was you,' he told the new arrivals.

'What's happening?'

'Hamel, the outlaw – he's busted loose from the rangers. Smashed one up pretty bad. He's lying low in the chaparral down there and the other ranger's got him trapped. You'd best get off those horses because there could be some stray lead flying around here soon.'

Martin thought quickly. 'Is anyone helping that ranger?'

'Hell, no, It ain't none of our business and that ranger's too big for his boots anyway. A bullet hole or two in him will do him the world of good.'

Martin said quietly to Owens, 'This could be our chance. We can ride down the street and slip between the houses. While one keeps the ranger busy, the other can get Hamel up behind him and gallop away.'

'Maybe Hamel won't want to get up behind one of us. I seem to recall he was fairly keen to avoid us.'

'He has more chance with us than he has with the law. He won't hesitate,' Martin told his companion. He continued, 'Being the low skunk that he is, he'll try to shake us off later, but we can keep an eye on him. Now, get on your horse and we'll try to get

Hamel away before someone decides to help that ranger.'

Hamel was crawling forward all senses alert for the first sign of his hunter. He had Marty's gun cocked in his hand and was watching for any sign of danger, but he expected that this would come in human form: he did not see the snake.

The reptile was perfectly camouflaged among the low scrub and shadows on the ground. It had been washed out of its hole by the flood and was feeling fearful in its unaccustomed surroundings. With the instincts of its kind, the snake lay perfectly still, at first relying upon its camouflage. But the danger did not stop or move away. As Hamel crawled forward, his extended hand holding the gun came perilously close to the hidden and by now thoroughly alarmed reptile. It struck savagely breaking its fangs on the barrel of the gun that had unintentionally been thrust near it. By sheer reflex action, Hamel squeezed the trigger. As the gun fired he threw himself away from the angry snake rolling sideways, hoping that it was not following.

Ben heard the shot and saw the chaparral thrashing violently about thirty yards in front and slightly downhill from where he had stationed himself. He snapped a shot at where he could see the bushes moving. Hamel's snarling face and his gun barrel appeared above the scrub and his Colt roared in reply. The bullet went nowhere near the ranger who changed position and fired again.

Suddenly a bullet whistled past his face and Ben saw that a rider had ridden out from between the houses, spurring his mount through the chaparral and spraying shots at him from a Winchester repeater. The horseman was out of effective revolver range, forcing the ranger to duck for cover among the bushes. Then he heard another horse smashing through the brush and a voice calling, 'Eric – over here!'

Chancing a bullet from the rifleman, Ben looked up and saw a man on a black horse barely fifty yards away. Hamel had abandoned his cover and was running towards the rider. He was almost to his rescuer when the ranger fired. The outlaw staggered but did not go down. The mounted man caught his right arm and swung him up onto the black's rump. As the horse turned away, Ben tried another shot but the hammer fell on a spent cartridge.

The rifleman snapped another shot at him but a moving horse is not a steady base for a shooter and the bullet missed. Another bullet cut a piece from the bush beside the ranger but this did not come from the horseman. Someone among the distant spectators was also firing at him. He heard shouts of drunken laughter and shots as bullets started striking in his general area. Dropping to the ground, Ben crawled downhill towards the houses, anger boiling within him.

Then a burst of gunfire erupted from the back windows of the hotel and he heard Josh Shelley bellowing, 'Clear off, you drunken scum!'

Taking advantage of the covering fire, Ben jumped to his feet and sprinted for the cover of the buildings. He could hear the horses pounding along the street as Hamel and his rescuers fled. Then there were more shots, this time from the front of the hotel. These shots were different. They had the sharp, spiteful bark of a small-calibre revolver.

Reloading as he ran, the ranger sprinted between a couple of derelict buildings and emerged on the street.

He saw that Hamel had fallen from the horse in front of the hotel and was struggling to rise. The rider who had originally rescued him was wheeling his horse about, taking shots at someone in the hotel as he called for the fallen outlaw to remount. Further up the street, a second horseman brandishing a gun, was trying to steady his nervous horse.

Having seen how easily a previous bullet had penetrated the hotel wall Ben felt a surge of apprehension. He remembered the small revolver in the hotel office and feared that it was Jane who had fired on the outlaws. He could only hope that the return fire had not hit her.

Resting his gun hand in the crook of his left elbow he sighted carefully at the man on the black horse in an attempt to divert his attention from the shooter in the hotel. But he was panting from his run and had trouble holding the weapon steady. Even as he squeezed the trigger, he knew he had missed though the hat flew from the horseman's head. That was enough for the would-be rescuer. Shouting curses at the man on the ground, the hatless one wheeled his mount, drove in the spurs and fled.

His companion waiting at the end of the street fired his carbine at Ben with no success and as soon as the other bandit reached him, they spurred their horses around the corner out of sight.

Ben ran to where Hamel lay bleeding. The back of his checkered shirt was soaked in blood and more was trickling from the corner of the outlaw's mouth. He was a ghastly colour, semi-conscious and mumbling incoherently as the ranger took him under the arms and dragged him onto the hotel veranda.

Jane appeared at the door reloading a small revolver, her face pale but determined. She looked at the wounded man and shuddered. In a small, shaky voice, she said quietly, 'I hope I haven't killed him, Ben.'

'You didn't. That was my bullet – hit him in the back just before he got on the horse. Looks like it busted up a lung pretty badly. You shouldn't have got involved, Jane. You could have been killed. These hotel walls won't stop .45 slugs.'

'I know,' she said. 'There are a few more holes in the walls. Pa will not be very happy.'

He turned his attention to the man on the ground. As the ranger sought to lift the wounded man's head, Hamel's rasping breath stopped abruptly. He shuddered slightly and then lay still. The State of Texas was saved the cost of a trial.

EIGHT

Missouri had taken no part in the haphazard gunplay that had erupted after Hamel's escape attempt. Santos had given him further work, the task of killing Ben Lawton, but the killer would do it in his own way at a time of his choosing. He had another job as well: Jane Shelley had foiled his first attempt to kill Grant; she would pay for that with her life. Exaggerated stories had circulated about how she had put the mysterious intruder to flight and these reflected badly upon Missouri's courage. He was determined that by the time he left Red Rock Crossing, his prestige would be restored and two more victims would be added to the dark legend that was growing around him.

Perched in the rafters of a ruined building and peering out through a hole in the roof, Missouri watched the activity at the hotel. He smiled as Pedro worked energetically with scrubbing brush, mop and bucket to wash Hamel's blood off the veranda floorboards. He thought of the work ahead and reckoned that the handyman would have a lot more practice at that particular task before the level of the San Tomas went down.

Inside the hotel there was great activity. The Shelley family had insisted that Ben move from the stables into the main building. Josh suspected that Hamel's men, unaware that he was dead, might try another rescue attempt with more men. They had learned that many of the people currently stranded by the flood, would not interfere. There was speculation too about the reappearance of the sinister masked intruder. Had he really been after Grant?

Ben had a busy time. He had to make an inventory of the property of both Grant and Hamel and arrange for their burials. The small settlement had no undertaker but a local handyman had developed the ability to construct rough coffins. After that the funeral had to be conducted by those connected with the deceased. The ground around the crossing was hard and stony so the locals buried their dead about half a mile from the town in an area out of the San Tomas valley.

Two stranded travellers, down on their luck, were only too happy to drive Grant's buckboard out to the cemetery and dig the graves. Ben paid them out of his own pocket but obtained a receipt so he could claim reimbursement later.

Marty was still drifting in and out of consciousness and the ranger feared that he might have suffered a fractured skull. Both his eyes were swollen and black and when he opened them in one of his conscious moments, they were just blood-shot slits.

Agnes had taken over nursing duties, bustling about with the confident air of someone who had seen worse cases. 'If he keeps rested,' she told the others, 'he should be all right. If the skull is fractured, it's not depressed. I remember that poor Woods boy who was kicked in the head by a horse. He had no chance, but I think that Marty will come right if his brain's not bleeding.'

Having an enforced wait because of the funeral arrangements, Ben suggested to Jane that they take a walk down to the crossing to see if the water level had fallen. It was an excuse for them to be together. Arm in arm they walked the short distance to the river. The flood had subsided but the water level was still dangerously high. Flood debris of all kinds was caught in some of the trees and bushes at the water's edge.

'Marty and I won't be needing the crossing now,' Ben said, as he looked across the brown water.

Jane pointed to the top of a red rock, just visible above the stream. 'That's the red rock that gave this crossing its name. There needs to be about another three feet of it visible before it is safe to cross. It could take another day yet.'

'We need to watch where we are walking, the floods always flush out plenty of snakes. I think Hamel might have crawled onto one yesterday. Something unusual made him fire his gun accidentally.'

The girl laughed. 'I've lived here all my life. I don't need. . . .' Her voice trailed off as she saw movement among the trees.

Ben followed her gaze. 'It's Gonzales,' he told her. 'He's camped in one of the derelict houses.'

The Mexican appeared, as usual carrying his old shotgun by the muzzle with the butt over his shoulder.

'No luck with the rabbits today?' the ranger greeted.

The Mexican gave a rueful smile. 'No rabbit but many snakes. I don't eat them.' Then, as if noticing Jane for the first time, he lifted his battered sombrero. '*Buenos dias, señorita.*'

Ben pointed to the old shotgun. It was a very battered 12 gauge. Its stock had been cracked and mended with rawhide, the barrel was lacking about eight inches and he could see a rear sight crudely soldered to it. 'That's an odd-looking gun you have there, Emilio. Looks like it's seen better days. Where did you pick that one up?'

'This gun, she got mud stuck in barrel, belled it out when its owner fired it. He was going to throw away but I tell him, give to me. I saw off the broken end and she shoot good enough. She no have a choke but good enough for me.'

'Who put the back sight on it?' Ben asked. 'Most shotguns don't have back sights.'

'I put on that sight, and the front one,' Gonzalez said proudly. 'Now I can shoot solid slugs and kill deer or buffalo.'

'If you can get close enough,' Ben reminded. 'Wouldn't a rifle be better?'

The Mexican gave a knowing smile. 'Gonzales, he can always get close enough. Is true I would prefer the rifle, but I can afford this gun.'

'I wouldn't like to get in the way of one of your twelve-gauge slugs,' the ranger observed.

Gonzalez gave a broad smile. 'I promise, *señor*, that I will not shoot you with a slug.'

Ben laughed. 'There are enough people who want to shoot me already. You would need to get on the end of a very long line.'

Martin and Owens were seated on rocks in the cave as they heated the last of the beans they had been carrying. The younger outlaw was dividing their last strip of jerky to eat with the beans. Both had spent the last hour bemoaning their bad luck. For a brief moment they had Hamel but then he had slipped through their fingers again.

'Do you reckon Hamel might still be alive?' Martin had asked the question several times in the last hour.

'Like I keep telling you – I don't know. I think he was hit pretty bad. He was making some strange noises just before he fell off the horse.'

'With him dead, we ain't got a chance of finding where he stashed the money. He was the only one could tell us.'

'There could be someone else who knows,' Owens suggested. 'What if he told them rangers in the hope of getting a lighter sentence?'

Martin spat. 'Eric Hamel was like an oyster. He told nobody nothing. You're barking up the wrong tree there.'

'Maybe not. They might have tortured the information out of him or maybe he talked to ease his conscience when he thought he was dying. Even if he's dead, that ranger might know more than he's prepared to tell.'

'Are you suggesting that we grab that ranger and make him talk? What if he won't talk or doesn't know anything?'

Owens allowed himself a tight little smile and produced a knife from his boot top. 'He'll talk if he knows anything. They all do when I go to work on them.'

Much to the relief of the Shelley family, the town handyman delivered two rough coffins so the dead men could be removed. Pedro and Rushton helped Ben load the corpses inside, and nailed them closed. Finally they put the coffins in a borrowed wagon which the ranger would drive. Rushton volunteered to go with the wagon to help the unloading and Waldren also appeared, Bible in hand.

'I feel that someone should say something over those men,' he said.

'Climb onto the wagon,' Ben told him. 'What

you'll say over them will probably be better than what's been said about them.'

They clattered out of town and up the long slope that led out of the San Tomas valley. The road had been badly damaged by the rain but the borrowed pair of half-Percherons leaned into their collars and they made good time up the slope. Topping the hill they could see a flat section some distance away with a wagon and men and horses standing nearby.

'Looks like Santos is up ahead,' the ranger observed. 'Probably planting Mandle. I didn't time this too well. There could be trouble here.'

'Surely not at a funeral,' Waldren sounded shocked.

'Some folks are not real fussy where they start trouble. I have to go on but if either of you gents want to jump out now, I won't hold it against you. It's not your fight.'

Rushton swallowed nervously, but then adopted a resolute tone. 'I owe you a favour – I'm going on.'

' "Blessed are the peacemakers".' Waldren raised his eyes skywards as he spoke. 'I'm going on.'

'I hope that blessing doesn't refer to the Colt Peacemakers Santos and his pals are carrying,' was Ben's grim observation.

Santos and a couple of his friends from Dawson's saloon were just shaping the final mound over Mandle's grave when they saw the ranger drive up. The big man scowled and muttered under his breath as the wagon halted beside the two open graves.

As he jumped from the wagon, Ben knew that trouble was not far away.

NINE

'So the killer's planting a couple more of his victims,' Santos sneered, as he saw the coffins in the wagon.

'One is mine, but I suspect that the other is yours, Santos,' Ben was not in a conciliatory mood. 'I know you didn't fire the shot that killed Grant but I'm sure you paid the man who did. When I can prove it, I'll be coming after you.'

'No doubt you'll shoot me in the back like you did Hamel.'

'I'll probably only see your back, Santos. You're not the type to face a man and fight.'

An angry scowl came across the big man's face, but he dared not try for his gun. Instead he reached down slowly to the buckle on his gunbelt. Counting on his advantage in height, weight and reach, he took a gamble. 'I'm a rancher not a gunman, but I doubt that you're game enough to meet me with bare fists.' To avoid giving the ranger an excuse to shoot him, Santos unbuckled his cartridge belt and lowered his holstered weapon to the ground. 'How tough are you without a gun?'

Ben turned to Rushton. 'Can you use a gun?'

The drummer replied, 'I don't carry one but I have used one.'

'Good,' the ranger said, as he unbuckled his gunbelt and passed his Colt to him. 'You have just been appointed the referee. Shoot any other sonofabitch who tries to join in the hostilities.'

'Don't do this, gentlemen,' Waldren pleaded. 'Have you no respect for the dead?'

Santos paused while rolling up his sleeves. 'Hell, I ain't got respect for half of the living,' he announced, ' 'specially a certain back-shooting skunk who hides behind a lawman's badge.'

'Don't do this, please, justice will prevail. The Lord will settle all accounts in His own time,' the preacher urged.

Santos glared at the little man. 'I ain't waiting that long. I intend to fix a few things right now.'

'Let's get this party started,' Ben said grimly, as he strolled out onto an open area of flat ground.

Santos quickly joined him, hunched his shoulders and charged in like a wild steer. He was much faster than the ranger had expected and Ben took a couple of hard blows on his forearms before skipping back out of range. Encouraged by the retreat, the rancher charged in again. This time he ran into a straight left. Ben felt the jar run up his arm and the slight sting as the skin on his knuckles split. Santos stepped back a pace, spat blood from where his lips had been mashed against his teeth and charged into the fray again. He threw a looping left that lifted a bit of skin from his opponent's forehead. It was only a glancing blow without the weight of his body properly behind it, but it warned Ben that the big man was a powerful puncher. Again, he skipped out of the way. He was prepared to give a bit of ground in order to study his adversary's style. He soon found that Santos was not particularly skilful. He was tough, prepared to take several punches to deliver one of his own and was relying upon his strength to outlast that of the man he was fighting. He would be a hard man to hurt.

Ben met the next rush with another straight left and again knew that it had done damage. In return he took a solid blow on the shoulder and just managed to deflect a huge, crashing right. Momentarily they came together in a clinch but the ranger backed away quickly. Smaller men are supposed to have the advantage inside a tall man's reach, but Santos, for all his slow feet, was quick with his hands. Any opponent would tire quickly if he tried to push against the bigger man's weight. No rules had been agreed upon and Ben did not want to be grabbed by the big rancher. Consequently he continued to retreat.

The pace of the first few minutes could not be maintained and soon both men were panting for breath. Briefly they circled each other and then Santos charged in again. He had run into Ben's left too often and now was unconsciously holding his

81

head back as he advanced. The ranger switched his attack ducking under his adversary's pawing punches and ripping a hard left into the man's short ribs. Involuntarily, Santos hunched over and his hands came down. Ben's left-hand attack changed to the exposed jaw and a savage hook had the rancher glassy-eyed and swaying on his feet. Dazed and with weary arms sagging, the big man was an easy target for a right cross that came over his guard. Ben knew that he risked injuring his gun hand by hitting Santos high on the head but it was a risk that he had to take. His fist smacked solidly against the bridge of the big man's nose. The rancher staggered back, snorted blood from his broken nose and charged in again. Ben hit him with another left but it failed to stop him. The big hands reached out and one caught the ranger's arm. With lightning speed Ben swung his free arm over those of Santos, half turned and drove his elbow backwards. The big man's head rocked under the impact, his grip relaxed and he staggered. By now he was half blinded by blood and his rapidly swelling eyes and probably never saw the powerful right-hander that his opponent had directed at his chin.

Ben knew that he had hit as hard as he could punch. The blow jarred up his arm but the effect on Santos left nothing to be desired. The rancher shot straight backwards raising a small cloud of loose dust as his body hit the earth. Unsure whether the fallen man could hear him, Ben said harshly, 'If you have any sense, Santos, you'll stay down. But there's more of the same if you reckon you ain't had enough.'

Santos rolled on his side and struggled to all fours. The urge to fight was still there but reason told him that continuation of the battle would only add to his considerable pain. Wearily he allowed himself to fall back to the ground.

Ben retrieved his gun and ordered the rancher's companions to load him into the wagon and take him back to town. They needed no urging for they were sure that the day's events would seem better after a visit to Dawson's saloon.

Aware that he would be stiff and sore when his body cooled, the ranger wasted no time with the burials. Rushton helped him lower the coffins into the graves and then they took a shovel each and started filling them in. Waldren read aloud from his Bible as the other two toiled. Had they not been so busy they might have wondered about the relevance of readings about Noah and the deluge but left that side of the burial to the preacher.

When their task was completed, all climbed into the wagon and headed for Red Rock Crossing. Soreness was beginning to set in and, as Ben drove the team, he realized that Santos had landed more blows than he had originally thought. By the time they reached town, he was aching all over.

Jane was suitably horrified at the state of Ben's face while her father eagerly sought details of the fracas. Agnes Shelley, with an air of resignation, appeared with her medical kit, sat the ranger in a chair and went to work on him. While she worked, she told Ben that Marty was fully conscious but was still having a little trouble remembering what had happened. She assured him that he would be fit to travel in a day or so. Agnes had seen similar cases before in her years on the frontier. She also invited the rangers to take spare rooms in the hotel now that they were relieved of the responsibility of a prisoner Her motives though were not altogether altruistic. The thought of their mysterious night visitor worried her and the presence of two rangers on the premises was most comforting.

Not far away, as night was falling, Missouri crouched in the ruin where he was living and began devising future plans. He had to kill Ben Lawton; Santos was paying him for that. But he also had to kill Jane Shelley for the sake of his own prestige. Being put to flight by a woman was harmful to the reputation he had worked so hard to achieve.

TEN

A couple of hours after darkness fell, his face masked and feet shod in moccasins, Missouri stole out again and, keeping to the brush behind the buildings, made his way to the back of the hotel. He paused at the stables long enough to ascertain that the rangers had moved into the main building. This arrangement pleased him in one way as he had more opportunities to move freely outside the hotel. Quietly he stole up to a lighted back window and peered through. The curtains were open slightly and through the gap he could see Agnes Shelley preparing food in a large crockery bowl. The sound of female voices came through the glass and by changing his position slightly, the watcher could see that Jane Shelley was also in the room. She appeared to be drying dishes that she took from a large tub of water.

Silently Missouri drew his revolver and cocked it. He would have preferred to kill the girl in some more spectacular manner but decided to take the opportunity that had presented itself, He eased back the hammer and sighted through the notch in it that did duty as a rear sight. He hoped that the window glass would not affect the bullet's flight. Just as his finger began to apply pressure to the trigger, Jane moved out of the killer's range of vision. Knowing by the voices that she was still in the room, he waited. For some minutes the girl was out of Missouri's range of vision as she went about various tasks. Cursing silently at the restricted view caused by the curtains, he waited.

Again she came into view and the waiting gunman lined his sights on the target.

Missouri did not know what came first, the heavy hand on his shoulder, or the desperate shout of, 'No!'

He whirled and fired into the dark form that had thrown an arm around him. The gun exploded and the shooter felt his attacker shudder. He fired twice more before the man reeled away and collapsed on the ground. Once again Missouri fled. Lacking the element of surprise, it was too dangerous to remain where he was and try for another shot at Jane. His survival depended upon stealth and a confrontation with armed men would quickly end his career.

Pedro, the stable hand, was gasping for breath and struggling to rise but the three bullets had done their work and he fell back to the ground with his heart arteries blasted apart.

Mother and daughter both screamed in alarm at

the shots outside the kitchen window. Ben heard the commotion and bounded down the stairs. He knew the firing had come from just behind the building. As he passed the kitchen door, he saw to his relief that both women were frightened but unharmed.

'Be careful,' Jane called. 'Someone's outside shooting.'

Ordering Jane to extinguish the lamp, Ben threw open the back door and launched himself into the darkness outside. He kept moving as his eyes tried to adjust to the change in light. He listened too for any sound that would indicate the shooter's presence,

An upstairs window, the sash swollen by the recent rain, squeaked open and Shelley called down, 'What's the shooting about?'

'I don't know, but be careful,' Ben shouted back.

The ranger took two more strides and his foot came into contact with something soft. Dropping to one knee, he felt before him and his hand touched clothing, coarse cloth sticky with what he knew would be blood.

'Bring a light – someone's been shot.'

Jane came through the back door carrying a lamp. The ranger was about to warn her of the danger when the light fell on the body on the ground. 'It's Pedro,' she gasped in horror. 'Is he dead?'

'He is – now leave the light and go inside. Whoever shot him is around here somewhere.'

An apparition in cowboy boots, a hat with bandages showing beneath it, and a nightshirt, was next on the scene. Marty was back in the land of the living and held a Winchester in his hands. 'What's happening?' he demanded.

'Someone killed Pedro and might still be out there. Move out of the light and keep watch while I drag him inside.'

It was hours later before those at the hotel finally retired. Ben had taken a lantern and examined where the man had been killed. The only boot tracks were those of the dead man but the ranger knew from the absence of a weapon that Pedro had not killed himself. The powder burns on the victim's clothing showed that he had not been shot from a distance and Ben was almost certain that the killer had worn moccasins. He remembered the sinister visitor of a couple of nights earlier and felt sure that it was the same person. Had he been after Pedro originally? It seemed highly unlikely. Chances were that the stable hand had accidentally encountered his murderer while returning from one of his many chores. As Grant was dead it seemed most likely that the killer was after at least one member of the Shelley family; the hotel's guests were unlikely to be his target. Rushton was a stranger to the area and only the two rangers knew that they would be escorting their prisoner via Red Rock Crossing.

Both rangers arose early next morning and searched the area where the murder had occurred. They found a moccasin track on a piece of soft ground and it was pointed downriver toward the ruined part of the town.

'I reckon the killer's using those ruins for a hide-out,' Marty said. 'I think we should have a few words with them that's camped there. Someone might have seen or heard something.'

Ben, stiff and very sore from the previous day's encounter, was not very optimistic. 'You're right, but I don't think that two of us could make much of a search. The best we can hope for is that someone there saw or heard something odd last night. They certainly would have heard the shots.'

The first people interviewed were Virgil and Homer Brown. The bootleggers were packing to leave and did not want the rangers looking too closely at the contents of their wagon.

'The river's down,' Homer announced, briskly, when he saw the lawmen arrive. 'Time we were on our way.'

'Just before you do,' Ben told him, 'I'd be mighty interested to hear what you know about last night.'

Both men admitted hearing the shooting but knew nothing of the murder. They thought that the shots had come from Dawson's saloon. Both denied seeing or hearing anything suspicious in their own surroundings. They had been at Dawson's for a short while on the previous night, but had seen a few of the regulars starting to get short-tempered and decided that it was best not to stay.

Neither ranger suspected the Browns of any involvement in Pedro's killing and had little interest in their other activities, but felt that they should make thorough enquiries. Virgil did not welcome any close scrutiny so hoped to divert the lawmen by revealing what he had overheard while in the saloon.

Quite casually he said, 'I reckon you should be looking for Missouri Sam for that murder – I heard he's in town.'

That statement certainly grabbed the rangers' attention

'Where did you hear that?' Ben demanded. He had heard of the killer but had never suspected that he was in Texas

Originally from Louisiana, he had gained notoriety as a ruthless guerrilla during the Civil War. When hostilities ceased, he did not turn to banditry as many of his comrades had. The stealthy trade of the hired killer was safer and paid just as well. Missouri stayed well in the background and only a few of his killings had been definitely attributed to him. Nobody knew his real name and few could say what he really looked like. He could appear as a well-dressed townsman or a rough frontier type and wherever he went, he left bodies behind him. His legend grew from satisfied clients who would recommend his services. He would respond to specially worded advertisements in certain newspapers and those who hired him were warned that his identity must be protected. Even tough men like Tony Santos kept his identity a secret for Missouri had sworn to kill anyone who identified him.

'There have been all sorts of wild stories about Missouri Sam,' Marty said. 'We need more than a saloon rumour to go on. As far as we know, he has never operated in Texas. I think we could be wasting our time looking for him.'

Ben disagreed. 'If stories about him are half true, he could have been working here in Texas and nobody would know. Lots of people just go missing and killings by persons unknown happen from time to time. We have both seen supposed suicides that looked suspicious. But how do we keep an eye out for someone that no one can identify?' He turned to Virgil and demanded, 'Just who was it reckoned Missouri was in town?'

Lying came easily to the older boot-legger. He had heard a drunken Tony Santos mumbling about the killer's presence, but gave a much safer reply. 'It was that feller you shot – that Mandle *hombre*. I heard him talkin' about it while he was drunk.'

'Did he say anything else about him?'

'No. He realized that he'd said too much and shut up.' At least that much had been true even if the identity of the person concerned had been concealed. Mandle was well beyond the killer's reach but Santos was alive and still very dangerous.

The rangers looked at each other. It was news they did not want to hear. If Brown could be believed, a new and deadly player had entered the game.

ELEVEN

Martin and Owens were hungry as well as frustrated. They had intended to buy supplies at Red Rock Crossing before attempting to free Hamel but the outlaw's abortive escape had altered all their plans. With little chance that they would succeed, the pair spent hours hatching plans to snatch Ben Lawton and find out what he really knew about Hamel's hidden loot. When they went to their blankets that night, they were able to ignore rumbling stomachs. The situation changed dramatically when they arose next morning.

'There ain't no other way,' Owens announced. 'We have to go to town to get some grub. We could probably grab that ranger while we're there.'

Martin chewed on a wad of tobacco for a while and eventually agreed. But, like his comrade, he had a few misgivings. They had heard that one ranger was laid up with a busted skull and by their own observations, it was unlikely that his partner could recruit other help in town. However, both men were conscious that they were taking a big chance.

The pair cleaned and checked their guns, mounted their horses and turned them toward Red Rock Crossing.

Marty and Ben continued their enquiries. They found Waldren seated on the front steps of a ruined house reading his Bible. His welcoming smile vanished when he heard the purpose of the rangers' visit. He closed the book. 'I must see the Shelleys. They might want me to conduct a funeral service for that poor man. He was like one of the family to them.'

'Just before you go,' Ben said, 'did you see or hear anything suspicious around nine o'clock last night?'

Waldren thought a while and shook his head. 'I don't own a watch but can't remember anything unusual. That Mexican feller, Gonzales, he's camped in the next building. He gets about a bit at night. He goes hunting rabbits and small game to eat. He might have seen something.'

'Didn't you hear three shots last night?' Marty asked suspiciously.

'I did, but was not sure where they came from. Thought it was those drunks at Dawson's acting up. The Lord will smite that place one day. It's only a matter of time.'

Fearing the onset of a sermon, the rangers left. In the next house they found Gonzales busy with an awl, needles and waxed thread, repairing a split in the upper of a very worn boot. He put down his work and sat against a wall wearing one boot with a much-holed sock on the other foot.

'Looks like you need a new pair of boots,' Ben observed.

The Mexican gave a rueful smile. '*Sí*. When I get work I will get some more but I do not think you are here to discuss boots.'

'You're right,' Marty told him. 'Were you here all last night? There's been a shooting at the hotel.'

'So that is what the shots were. I was out on the river-bank where I had set some snares for rabbits. I hear shooting but take no notice. Much shooting happens at Dawson's saloon. I take no notice.'

'Do you go to Dawson's saloon much?' Ben remembered seeing Gonzales there on his last visit.

The Mexican shook his head. 'Not much – not enough money. Sometimes if I shoot ducks or rabbits I sell them to the cantina cook, but I don't drink much. When I fix this boot I will try to get another rabbit for my dinner.'

The ranger continued, 'When you were there, did you see any strangers?'

'Gonzales is stranger, too. How would I know who lives in this town?'

Ben persisted. 'While you were there did you hear anything about a man called Missouri?'

Gonzales looked blank. 'This Missouri – she is river. I know no man of that name.'

'So you saw nothmg unusual last night?'

'I saw that the river is down. But my horse, she needs a few more days on good grass, then I must be going.'

The rangers had not expected many results and knew that they must extend their enquiries further to Dawson's saloon.

The proprietor, as usual, was not happy to see any lawmen, but afforded Ben a little more respect after seeing the mess he had made of Santos. However he gave little away. He denied knowing anything about Missouri Sam's presence although he knew of the man's reputation. He, too, had never heard of the killer operating in Texas.

'Where's Santos?' Ben demanded. He reasoned that if Mandle knew about Missouri, there was a good chance that the big rancher would know.

'He's in that adobe jacal out the back. He's still a bit of a mess. I don't reckon he wants to see you.'

'That's nice to know,' Ben said. 'I think we might have a word with him.'

They found Santos on a bunk in a room that reeked of whiskey and tobacco. His face was a mess with lips swollen and split and both blackened eyes reduced to mere bloodshot slits that had swelled past the bridge of a flattened nose. When he heard the ranger's voice, Santos fumbled for the holstered six-gun beside the bunk.

'Leave that right where it is, Santos. You could say this is a social call, but if you go for that gun I'll kill you.'

The battered man took the hint, sat up and snarled through puffed lips, 'What do you want, Lawton?'

Ben told him what he had heard but Santos claimed to know nothing. He even ventured the opinion that Mandle used to make all sorts of claims when he was drunk. Though he did not know who had informed the rangers, he was pleased that they had the wrong name and had not directly involved him. He even went so far as to suggest that he would have no reason to bring in an outside killer. 'I catch and kill my own,' he snarled.

The rangers reminded him that he was in Red Rock Crossing for the express purpose of killing Grant and, until they were convinced otherwise, he was considered a suspect.

'Missouri might have fired the shot,' Marty told him, 'but someone else made the bullet.'

'If that's the case, why would I want to kill that Mex stable hand?' Santos mumbled.

'I don't know but sure as hell I mean to find out,' Ben told him.

The sunlight was glaring after the dark room and both rangers blinked a little as they emerged into the harsh light. Only one person was stirring on the street. It was Gonzales walking towards the river-bank with his old shotgun over his shoulder.

'He's leaving things a bit late in the day to go hunting,' Marty observed.

'Ain't much else to do around here,' Ben

muttered. 'The Shelleys are burying Pedro this afternoon but apart from that not much seems to be happening. I was talking to Rushton this morning. The river's down and he's pulling out today, too. We need to get to a telegraph to tell Captain McNeil what's happened here and see what he wants us to do.'

'He won't be too happy the way things have turned out. The nearest telegraph is at Three Mesas over the river.'

Ben thought for a while and eventually suggested, 'Why don't you go there with Rushton in his buggy? You could hitch your horse behind for the ride back. There's a doctor there so you can get him to have a look at your head and you can get our new instructions over the telegraph.'

Marty liked the idea but still had a few misgivings. 'Sounds like a good idea to me. But what about you? There could be trouble here while I'm away.'

Ben said that he was worrying needlessly. Hamel's associates had fled and Tony Santos was recuperating and had developed a whole new respect for the law.

'That still leaves Missouri,' Marty reminded.

'We're not sure that he is here, and even if he is, he would not be after me.'

'Don't bet your life on that. We make a lot of enemies in this job.'

An hour later, Marty left town with Rushton. He was glad to be out of Red Rock Crossing. He disliked the town and three days there had seemed much too long.

Missouri watched the ranger leave and allowed himself a grim smile.

TWELVE

Martin and Owens rode into Red Rock Crossing in mid-afternoon. Though both were keen to have a drink, they shopped for supplies first and Owens bought himself a new grey hat to replace the one that Ben had shot off his head. At the general store they bought a small supply of bacon, coffee, beans, canned fish and a few cracker biscuits. Lacking a pack animal, they could not carry much and carefully divided their purchases into their respective saddle-bags. Years on the wrong side of the law had taught them to do the most necessary tasks first in case they had to leave town in a hurry.

Their next stop was the cantina. The cook was not happy about preparing food at such an odd hour but thought it best to comply. He knew dangerous men when he saw them. When their meal was finished, they made their way to Dawson's saloon.

Dawson knew them, though for the benefit of the other patrons, he pretended otherwise. As he poured their drinks, he said quietly, 'You boys are taking a risk here. There's a ranger in town.'

'That's good,' Martin said casually. 'Only one?'

'The other left town this morning. Looked like he was going to Three Mesas.'

Owens sipped his drink, thought a while and asked, 'Where would we find this other ranger?'

'He's over at Shelleys' hotel – could be there on his own. I saw the Shelleys leaving town about an hour ago. They were going to the bone yard to plant a feller who got shot last night. They were pretty cut up about it. He'd worked for them for a long time.'

'So there's no one else around?' Martin asked. He had not expected such luck.

'There could be a down-at-heel Mexican, or a crazy preacher, but they won't cause any problems. They're camped in those derelict buildings on the other side of the hotel. Be careful about taking on that ranger though. He's one tough *hombre*.'

Owens said dismissively, 'He might be tough but he ain't bullet-proof.'

Martin threw down his drink and said to his partner, 'Let's go. We need to have a word with that ranger.'

Dawson shook his head in disbelief. 'You're loco, the pair of you.'

Ben was tired. He had not had much sleep and dozed as he sat in a chair on the hotel veranda. Suddenly it became too much of an effort to read the newspaper he had and he dropped it onto his lap, put his feet on the veranda rail and tipped his hat over his eyes. He saw no danger in taking a short nap.

Missouri was lurking in the trees along the river-bank. Santos had paid him to shoot the ranger and here was the ideal opportunity, a clear shot at an unsuspecting target at a time when there was nobody to interfere. He slipped another bullet into the breech and raised his weapon. Then he swore silently. Two men had moved between him and his victim.

Ben awoke with a start. He was never sure if it was the sound of approaching footsteps or the cocking of a revolver that brought him out of his sleep. Two men stood on the road before him with guns in their hands.

'Don't reach for that gun,' Martin ordered. He needed to take the ranger alive but Ben did not know that.

'Just stay right where you are,' Owens snarled. 'We need to have a little talk about what Hamel did with the money from our last job.'

Missouri watched in dismay. Ben was his victim. If he did not kill him, Santos would want his money back. Worse, too, his reputation would suffer. He had no doubt that the pair with guns intended to shoot the ranger so decided that he would have the first shot. He could see his target through a space between the two gunmen. Carefully he squinted down the sights, centred them on Ben's blue shirt and took up the slack in the trigger. Even as the hammer fell, he saw that one of the gunmen had stepped in the way.

Martin spun sideways as the .44 bullet hit him in the nape of the neck.

Ben only half comprehended what had happened, but, as he heard the shot and saw the stricken man fall across in front of his partner, he rolled off the chair and went for his gun. For once in his life, Owens reacted slowly and glanced about quickly seeking the other shooter. Then his instincts warned him that Ben was his greatest danger. By the time he turned back to the ranger, the latter had fired his first shot through the veranda rails. The bullet was hastily aimed and only plucked at the gunman's sleeve as it passed. His return shot shattered one of the upright railings and buried itself in the floor beside the ranger.

Ben fired again and this time his bullet struck home. Owens staggered and fired another wild shot but it failed to score. The ranger's gun roared almost simultaneously and this time Owens went down with a bullet in the forehead. He was probably dead before he hit the ground.

Missouri fired at Ben again but the ranger, still on the floor, was half obscured by a thick upright post and the vertical railings. All the shot did was to warn the ranger that the mystery shooter was no friend. Angry at failing again, the killer fired another shot and departed the scene.

Ben was still studying the trees for any sign of the shooter when he heard the heavy report of a shotgun. He had been surprised that the last rifle shot seemed to have hit nothing. It was then he remembered that Gonzales had been hunting along the river-bank with his shotgun. Moments later the Mexican appeared from the trees trying to reload his shotgun as he ran. He was also looking back fearfully over his shoulder. Then, appearing to notice Ben for the first time, he changed course slightly and ran to him.

Panting heavily, the Mexican halted. 'In the trees – a man with a gun. I see him shoot at you. I shoot at him with my shotgun but was too far away – Gonzales only has light shot in his cartridges. He has Winchester rifle. I run away.'

'You did the right thing and helped keep him from shooting me. Thank you for that. Now, get inside the hotel and keep watch through a window. I'm going to get my carbine and I'm going after that sonofabitch.'

'These dead men—' Gonzales pointed to the bodies. 'What we do about them?'

'Leave them for the time being. They can't do any more harm. What did that man who shot at you look like?'

'He had dark clothes. There was a black mask over his head. It happened too quick. I just see him through bushes. I shoot, then I run quick.'

Just then Waldren appeared around the side of the building. His face was flushed as if he had been hurrying. Seeing the dead men in the street, he stopped in horror and raised his eyes skywards. 'When, oh Lord,' he groaned, 'will men stop this madness?' Then he fell to his knees and began praying beside the bodies.

Curious heads appeared from around doorways after the shooting had ended and some customers from Dawson's emerged to inspect the damage. Cautiously the group walked over to the preacher and the two dead men and looked around.

'Leave that where it is,' Waldren said sternly, as one of the more opportunistic spectators sought to appropriate one of the fallen revolvers. The man grumbled something about the dead man no longer needing the weapon but did not persist in his plan.

Ben emerged from the hotel carrying his carbine. He told Waldren to secure the dead men's belongings and then hurried away to the river-bank. He doubted if the shooter would still be there but wanted to see his tracks before too many others walked over the scene.

He quickly found the three empty shells and looked in vain for footprints. He saw where the Mexican's broken boots had left prints in the still-damp soil but that was all. He was not surprised though. There were plenty of rocks in the area and the killer the night before had worn moccasins. He would be cautious about leaving tracks that could be followed.

The Shelley family had returned from Pedro's funeral before Ben decided to abandon his hunt for signs of the killer. The women, red-eyed and subdued, stayed inside, but Shelley himself came out and helped Ben make an inventory of the dead gunmen's possessions. The ranger identified them as the last of the Hamel gang and quietly marvelled at how lucky he had been because the shot that had killed Martin had surely been intended for him.

The town handyman, a lanky Negro named Abner Derby almost despaired when he found he had two more coffins to build. The work paid well but he was running out of suitable timber. He was forced to use boards pulled from derelict buildings and work late into the night to complete the task. Fortunately Derby had two large, strong sons and they quickly volunteered to go out to the cemetery and dig two more graves for the sum of one dollar each. Ben would pay the Derbys from the money the dead men had been carrying.

The ranger had his evening meal with the Shelley family but was not very good company. He was only half listening to the conversation and seemed deep in thought. Aware that he had killed a man that day, his hosts made allowances for his behaviour. They did not know the real reason for the frown on his face.

His own narrow escape and the gunfight that followed were not his main concern. Ben was worried most about the murder of Pedro. It made little sense that a hired killer should go after a quiet-living, Mexican stable hand. Both Jane and Gonzales had described the same man: he was sure of that. If it was the shadowy Missouri, his mission was more than just the murder of Grant. A professional killer would not risk killing a lawman unless he was being well paid to do so. Who was putting up the money?

The only link that Ben could find between himself and Grant was that both had made an enemy of Tony Santos. He knew, too, that if stories were right, Santos could afford to pay to have him murdered. But, like a rock in his boot, Pedro's seemingly pointless murder worried him more than the attempt on his own life.

Twice Jane had been close to an unknown intruder, someone who in one case, was prepared to kill. The circumstances were not similar but Ben was not sure that they had been coincidental.

He found the girl in the hotel office busily rearranging some ledgers on a shelf. She turned quickly as she heard the ranger's footsteps,

'Sorry if I frightened you,' Ben said.

The girl laughed nervously. 'I'm getting easy to frighten these days. After seeing that horrible man in the black mask, I've become quite jumpy. I'm almost certain he was behind Pedro's murder. What if he was outside the kitchen window when Pedro accidentally disturbed him? He might not have been after Pedro. He could have been after one of our family. It scares me to think that he might come back tonight.'

'I don't want to add to your worries, but stay scared

because you might be right. We have a killer loose here somewhere. He might be a complete madman who will be happy just to kill someone, or he might be here for a special purpose. It was only an accident that he shot Martin. I'm sure he was aiming at me. That's to be expected. I make enemies in this job, but he could also be after you or your parents too. Do you have a gun handy?'

Jane opened a desk drawer and removed a Colt Cloverleaf house pistol. 'I have this.'

Ben shook his head. 'Those .41 rim-fire cartridges won't stop much. They're made for cheap guns with poor quality metal in them and there's too small a charge behind them. Owens had a .38 hideout gun on him. I'll loan it to you. The revolver is only about the same size as the one you have there, but it hits a lot harder. I want you to carry it with you at all times. Don't stand near lighted windows at night or stand in doorways, and tell your parents the same.'

'So you think we could be in danger? I thought I was worrying myself unnecessarily.'

'I don't like being an alarmist, but our mysterious friend is hanging about this hotel too much. I think he's after someone else as well as me but I don't know why. I'd hate anything to happen to you.'

Jane smiled and said with a laugh, 'Ben Lawton, I think you are actually concerned about me.'

'You could be right there,' the ranger admitted.

Away from prying eyes in a gloomy corner of a ruined house, Missouri cleaned his rifle barrel and

107

quietly cursed his run of bad luck. Failure put pressure on reasoning that had long been distorted by a lust to kill and a pride taken in cold-blooded murder. It rankled him that as one of the most feared men of the Kansas/Missouri border wars, he had been forced to flee by a girl and an unarmed one at that. She had to die. Santos had already paid him half this fee for killing the ranger and he too would die: Missouri was sure of it.

Santos wanted to see him. A piece of a bush hanging on a fence behind the saloon told him so. It was their agreed-upon signal and that night they would meet at 10 p.m. when they had the cover of darkness. He was not sure what Santos wanted but suspected that the rancher was growing impatient.

Missouri was growing impatient too. He was sick of Red Rock Crossing and the role that he was forced to play. It was getting harder as the days dragged by; the killer wanted to be someone else in some new location. He hoped that before the night was out Jane Shelley or the ranger, preferably both, would be dead.

THIRTEEN

The meeting with Santos was brief. The battered rancher was in no mood to mince words. He had paid to have Ben Lawton killed and was expecting results in the very near future. Missouri came away from the meeting seething with anger. He felt that Santos had not treated him with the respect he deserved and briefly considered killing him to teach him a lesson. But then he knew that such a move could be bad for business. No one would hire a killer if he thought that the hireling might later turn on him. As he quietly made his way back to his camp, Missouri knew that he would have little rest that night.

Business had picked up at the hotel. Aware that the river was falling three more travellers had used the Red Rock trail and had halted for the night on their journey north.

Ben had been busy too, caring for the horses. He had his own and those of the dead outlaws. He had moved the animals into the corral so that the hotel guests could use the stables for their horses. The moon was waning but with the clouds gone, it threw enough light for him to see to his work without the need for a lantern. He knew that Jane would be waiting for him in the hotel office and waited impatiently for the horses to finish eating. He did not want any of them injured fighting over food. The bay horse that Hamel had ridden was inclined to bully other horses if it finished eating first. He was standing quietly in the corral, his figure blending with the gate post when he saw movement in the shadows by the stable. Though he could not see very well, he was sure that it was a man.

Easing his Colt from its holster, Ben crooked his right thumb over the hammer ready to pull it back and fire. The dark shape seemed to glide eerily silent across the ground. Already the stranger was in long revolver range for night shooting, but the ranger was still unsure whether the person had any evil intent.

'Who's that?' he called.

The dark figure spun rapidly, a red muzzle flash stabbed toward him and something smacked solidly against Ben's jaw. Staggering back, he triggered a shot in the gunman's direction but it was badly aimed and went wide. Ignoring the stinging pain in his cheek, he sought his target again but the shooter was already around the corner of the stables. Though his first impulse was to run after the gunman, experience told Ben that he could also run onto a gun muzzle. A man who shot so well at night would be unlikely to miss at close range. With this in mind he paused and listened for any sounds of retreating footsteps but heard none. The unknown assailant was either long gone or lurking in ambush.

'What's going on?' Josh Shelley called from an upstairs hotel window.

'Be careful,' Ben shouted back. 'Someone just took a shot at me. Don't come out – and keep every-one away from the windows.'

Missouri cursed under his breath. He had missed Lawton. The element of surprise was gone. It was time to disappear.

The ranger stayed in the shadows and worked wide of the stable's corner. There was enough light for him to see that the unknown gunman was gone. A single man would have little chance of finding his attacker so he reluctantly gave up the hunt. With a sore and bleeding face, he entered the hotel where the Shelleys and several apprehensive guests were waiting.

'You're hit,' Jane said in alarm. 'Sit down here on the couch.'

'I'm lucky. It's only a graze, but whoever it was didn't miss by much.'

Agnes appeared with her medical kit. She sent Jane for a bowl of hot water while she examined the wound. Finally she announced, 'That's not a bullet graze, it's a wooden splinter.'

'The shot must have hit the corral post beside me and drove a splinter into my face,' Ben explained.

111

'I've been lucky.'

Jane arrived with the hot water and a clean cloth. Under her mother's directions she carefully cleaned the congealed blood away to reveal the end of a large splinter protruding from the ranger's cheek.

Agnes frowned. 'Corrals are bad places for blood poisoning so I need to get all of that splinter out.' She produced a pair of tweezers. 'Hold still, Ben, I have to get this all out in one piece. if it breaks I might have to cut out the broken piece. Now – don't move.'

Very carefully Agnes gripped the protruding end of the splinter and steadily withdrew it. Ben dared not move although the process was quite painful. The blood flowed again as the splinter came free. Holding it to the light Agnes examined it and told the others that nothing had broken off it. Then she sloshed spirit onto the wound. The patient winced with the burn of it but felt greatly relieved. Many a cowhand had died of lockjaw because of minor injuries sustained in corrals. None was sure why this happened but prompt attention seemed to be the best way to avoid a fatal infection.

People were still standing around discussing the night's happenings when Waldren hurried into the hotel, his Bible clutched in his hand. 'I heard shooting,' he announced. 'Are my services needed?'

'They will be when I catch up with a certain sonof—' Just in time Ben remembered that there were ladies in the room.

The preacher looked closely at the sticking plaster on the ranger's cheek. 'Have you been shot?'

'No. A bullet knocked a splinter off a post alongside me and it hit me in the face.'

'Praise the Lord, my young friend. You've had a narrow escape.'

'Did you happen to notice anyone around those empty houses before you came up here?' Ben asked.

Waldren rubbed the grey stubble on his chin and thought a while. 'Yes, I did. I saw that Mexican, Gonzales. He seemed to be in a hurry, said he had been checking on his horse. It struck me though, that night was hardly the time to be doing it. I would hate to do the man an injustice but there is something strange about him.'

And you, too, Ben thought. A preacher who knew so little about the Bible and who always seemed to be on the scene was raising his suspicions. Was he trying to steer him in the wrong direction? He resolved that tomorrow he would begin new enquiries based on the premise that the preacher was not all that he appeared to be. At present he was prepared to keep an open mind about Gonzales. When Marty returned he would begin a thorough search of the ruined part of town because he was sure that it concealed something that would lead him to the mysterious gunman. As yet the ranger could only guess at his identity.

Ben had retired to his room when he heard a horse halt outside the hotel and an urgent knocking on the front door. He picked up his revolver and

113

went out into the corridor. There he met Shelley who was also carrying a gun. Together they descended the stairs.

Standing clear of the door, Lawton demanded, 'Who's there?'

The late caller turned out to be a lad from Three Mesas who had an urgent message for Ben. It was from Marty. His telegraphed report to Captain McNeil had received a response directing him to wait in Three Mesas until joined by Rangers Harris and Bell. Then all would ride hard for Red Rock Crossing where they would make a thorough search for Missouri Sam.

Shelley gave the messenger a meal and a bed for the night. The boy would begin his return journey at first light the next day.

Aware that much-needed help was on the way, Ben slept a little easier that night.

FOURTEEN

The ranger was up early next morning. He wrote a note to Marty that he gave to the messenger and sent the rider on his way. Returning to the scene of the previous night's shooting, he examined the ground but learned nothing from it except that his would-be assassin wore moccasins. He found a print in a patch of mud.

With nothing better to do, he saddled his horse and took it out for an exercise. After days of idleness the chestnut was eager to go and stepped out briskly while his rider studied the landscape around the town. Behind the hotel, on the cemetery road, there were a couple of acres of fenced land with a small stream trickling through. Its neglected appearance indicated that the land's owner had long departed but two animals were grazing on the lush grass that grew there.

One was a brown mule. A bar burned through the US brand on its shoulder indicated that it had been cast from the army. Ben guessed that it would be

Waldren's mount. Such an animal was not the type that a hired killer would use for a quick escape, but a man like Missouri would not be averse to stealing a better mount if he needed one.

A mud-coated grey horse grazed nearby. Its tail was short and uneven in length and its mane looked as though other horses had chewed it at some time. Its head was buried in the long grass and was eating hungrily. Ben remembered Gonzales saying that he wanted to leave his horse on the good feed for a few more days before resuming his journey. It appeared to be filling out, with lean quarters but no sharp hips. Viewed head-on it was fairly ordinary in appearance but looked to be in good condition. He guessed that the Mexican would soon be on his way.

The ranger was enjoying his ride in the fresh morning air but felt that he should have been doing more to investigate the recent happenings. He was about to turn back towards town when he saw a rider approaching from that direction. To his delight, he recognized Jane astride a pretty buckskin pony. The combination was easy on the eye and suddenly he decided that Tony Santos and even Missouri, could wait.

'What are you doing away from the hotel so early?' Ben asked, when the girl stopped her pony beside his mount.

'I saw you riding out and thought that you might get lost out here on your own,' the girl laughed.

'You could be right,' the ranger admitted with a

smile. 'These days I need somebody to hold my hand.'

Talking and laughing they rode together to the high ridge that overlooked the town from the south. Below them they saw that the place was yet to come to life. Smoke rising from chimneys indicated that breakfasts were being prepared but there was no movement on the streets.

Missouri saw the riders on the ridge as he peered through gaps in the shingle roof of the ruin where he was living. It was his custom to survey the scene from his perch in the rafters before venturing out each day. He recognized Ben's horse, but because of the distance was unsure of the other rider's identity. When they turned their horses' heads to return to town, the killer saw that he would get a clear shot at the ranger as he came down the hill that led to the crossing. With the agility of a monkey he swung down from the rafters and hurried to get his rifle. A minute later he was back, slipping a cartridge into the breech as he sought a good firing position. Eventually he found one and rested his left hand on the weathered shingles to steady the barrel as he took aim. He knew that the weapon would throw high if he rested it on a hard surface.

Slowly they came into range and Missouri recognized Jane as the second rider. She too had been marked for death. He was pleased to note that the angle of his shot gave him a better target. If he missed one person, he would most likely hit the other. Ben was closest to the hidden gunman and was the most dangerous from his point of view but a hit on the girl would give him time to revert to his harmless bystander role. The ranger would not rush off and leave her if she was shot. Normally Missouri would not have attempted such action in daylight but he was quick to take advantage of the unexpected opportunity while few witnesses were about.

The foresight almost covered the ranger's upper body but the shooter knew that he would hit one of his targets though there would be little opportunity for a second shot.

He cocked the hammer, took a deep breath, leaned into the butt of the rifle and squeezed the trigger.

FIFTEEN

The bullet buzzed over Ben's head a fraction of a second before he heard the report of the gun.

'Down!' he shouted to Jane almost pushing her from the saddle while dismounting himself. 'Get behind your horse.'

'Who's shooting?' Jane was just coming to terms with what had happened.

Before replying Ben threw an arm around her waist and hauled her none too gently out of the saddle. 'I didn't see where the shot came from,' he replied, 'but I think it came from the town somewhere. Keep behind your horse.' With those instructions, the ranger drew his Winchester from its saddle scabbard and peered out under his horse's neck. Experience told him that the shot had come from the town but the echoes in the valley had made it difficult to pinpoint the sound of the report.

No tell-tale cloud of powder smoke was visible and at ground level he could only see the second storey of the hotel or the roofs of the ruined houses. The mystery sniper did not fire again. He had missed his opportunity and now was reluctant to disclose his position. The ranger led his horse forward so that it completely screened the girl and together they made their way down the hill.

Missouri swore angrily as he climbed down from his perch. A rotten shingle had given way when he leaned on it as he squeezed the trigger. As he sought to regain his balance, the shot had gone high. He was lucky not to have fallen from the rafters and injured himself but the killer did not see this. To his mind, his run of bad luck at Red Rock Crossing was continuing. He knew now that the ranger would come looking for him and briefly he considered another ambush but decided against it. An alerted ranger would not be easy to kill. He had survived so long by using his brains. Now was not the time for a confrontation.

Jane had drawn the revolver Ben had given her from the pocket of her riding skirt. Recent events had brought out a determination in her and she was prepared to hit back if she had to. Peering across the horses, the girl looked in the direction of the town but could see nothing.

When the buildings and the contours of the land concealed them from the hidden gunman, the pair remounted and rode briskly to the hotel. Sending the girl inside, Ben stabled the horses.

Tony Santos had heard the shot and, from his window, saw the couple take refuge behind their horses. With increasing frustration, he knew that Missouri had missed again. He also knew that he would draw suspicion on himself if he delayed too long at Red Rock Crossing. He would have to go home soon and leave the killing of Lawton to Missouri, but was beginning to suspect that the assassin's reputation had been exaggerated.

Squinting through his bruised and bloodshot eyes, he walked outside and angrily tore a small limb from a nearby cottonwood tree. Then he walked thirty yards to the fence and hung the branch on it. Missouri would see the signal and meet him at 10 p.m. that night. They had much to discuss and the rancher's patience was wearing thin. After that he stalked into the saloon and glared around as if challenging anyone to make a remark about his battered face.

Dawson wisely made no remark and his henchman, Jasper, took the lead from his boss.

'Good to see you up and around, Tony.' If Santos noted any false heartiness in Dawson's greeting, he made no comment.

'Come and have a drink,' Jasper invited. He knew that Dawson would return his money later. With a ranger in town it paid to have allies.

Meanwhile Ben was pacing about in frustration. He knew that the mystery gunman was still in town and that he would have little chance of finding him on his own. A man who knew the layout of the empty houses could play hide-and-seek with him and even lure him into an ambush. It worried him too that the killer of Grant and Pedro seemed to be paying too much attention to Shelley's Hotel. Who was he after?

His mood did not improve when Waldren joined him on the hotel veranda. The preacher waved his battered Bible and lamented the presence of evil that seemed to be stalking the town. He had heard of the attempted shooting and recalled hearing the shot. He said that he had been reading his Bible on the river-bank.

'Do you have any idea of where it came from?' Ben asked.

Waldren thought a while. 'It's hard to tell the way it echoed from the hills around. It could have come from one of those empty houses.'

'How many people are camped there now?'

'So far as I know, there's only that Mexican, Gonzales, and myself. I don't see much of him and he keeps to himself, but there's something strange about that man. At times his accent does not seem to be quite so Mexican.'

'Does he own a rifle?'

'I have only ever seen him with an old shotgun but there are many places where he could hide a rifle,' Waldren replied. 'I don't know what it is but there is something strange about him. I could be doing the man an injustice and if I am, I hope the Lord will forgive me, but something is not quite right with Gonzales. We have our animals in the same pasture and I often see him around but he keeps to himself too much.'

Ben could understand the Mexican giving Waldren a wide berth but later he asked Jane what she knew of the Mexican. She had seen him arrive at the crossing and was certain that he did not have a rifle. He was carrying his shotgun in a leather loop on his saddle horn. She was equally certain that Waldren also had not been carrying a rifle when he arrived.

The idea came to Ben that if someone in Red Rock Crossing had imported a hired gunman, he might have had a rifle waiting for him. He also had the notion that Pedro's murder might not have been a random crime. Had he died as the result of a Mexican feud? If he had, Gonzales seemed the logical suspect.

When questioned, Josh Shelley could give no motive for his employee's murder. Pedro had been with the family for years and was a temperate man who stayed out of trouble. Ben could only conclude that the Mexican had disturbed his murderer at the wrong time.

He was still racking his brain when he heard horses in the street and men talking.

SIXTEEN

Marty and Rangers Matt Harris and Stanley Bell climbed down from their weary horses in front of the hotel. They had been riding hard and their horses stood heads down and lathered with sweat when the trio dismounted.

Harris was a long, beanpole of a man in his mid-thirties, his height accentuated by his high-crowned black sombrero. He had been a ranger for several years but his occasional whiskey-inspired outbreak had slowed his promotion. Because of the other's height, Bell, his neatly dressed companion, looked small beside him. He was several years younger but had proved his worth in many a tight situation. A long-barrelled Colt rode on each of the ranger's hips but his air of stern authority was contradicted somewhat by his youthful appearance which he tried to conceal with a large moustache. Both men were handy with their guns and Ben could not have wished for more reliable reinforcements.

Marty seemed fully recovered from his injury and

was keen to get back to work. Later, at the corral, as the trio fed and groomed their horses, they informed their companion of the latest developments. Information received by Ranger Headquarters had revealed that Missouri Sam was believed to be in Texas and Captain McNeil had wasted no time in beginning the hunt for him.

Little was known about their quarry. A man of medium height and appearance, with dark eyes and aged in his forties, he had used several aliases but occasional survivors of the border wars had identified him only as Missouri Sam. Some who might have been able to identify the killer maintained a discreet silence. Those who claimed to know the former guerrilla often met mysterious deaths shortly afterwards. It was safest to forget what the man looked like. Lawmen from Missouri to Utah suspected him of several murders and so far as was known, he had stayed clear of Texas. Despite siding with Missouri in the border wars, some said that originally he had been a Cajun from Louisiana. Unfortunately, truth and legend had become entwined over the years and this considerably hampered the search for him.

'Presuming the description is right,' Ben told the others, 'I know two men here who could be our man. One is a Mexican and the other is a crazy preacher. There could be others too, hanging around that rats' nest that Dawson calls a saloon.'

'How do you reckon we should play this?' Marty asked.

Ben turned to Harris who was the most experienced ranger. 'What would you do, Matt?'

The lanky one drew on his cigarette for a second and eventually drawled, 'I reckon I'd make sure first who this Missouri Sam ain't. I'd look over Dawson and his friends, maybe hassle them a bit and see what they know. This character don't kill folks out of the kindness of his heart: someone's paying him.'

'That could be Tony Santos. He had a reason to have Grant murdered and after I improved his manners at the expense of his looks, he might have switched Missouri onto me. But I don't see why he was lurking around Shelley's Hotel.'

Marty gave the others a knowing wink. 'Maybe he thought that was where you were most likely to be lurking.'

'I saw that Shelley girl once,' Bell chuckled. 'You'd be a damn fool if you weren't making a play for her.'

'All this ain't catching Missouri Sam,' Ben growled defensively.

It took a while but finally the rangers agreed on a plan. Tomorrow they would swoop on the saloon and interview everyone there. When they were satisfied that no more was to be learned, they would search the derelict buildings and question Gonzales and Waldren.

Missouri was waiting in the darkness when Santos slipped out the back door of the saloon. A faint whistle brought the big rancher to a couple of pecan trees and he could just distinguish a dark shape pressed against one of the trunks.

'What do you want?' murmured a low voice.

'I want that Lawton sonofabitch dead. That's what I want and I seem to remember paying you to do it. Why is he still alive?'

'He's had the devil's own luck so far, but I'll get him. It might take a day or two. Three more rangers rode in today. Two of them might just be passing through. I can't do anything till I know what they're up to.'

'I can't hang around this blasted hole in the ground much longer and I want that ranger dead before I leave,' Santos snarled.

'I'll get him,' Missouri promised. 'I could let him go for a couple of weeks and then take him one dark night. Nobody would ever suspect you.'

'Like hell you will – I want to *see* that sonofabitch dead. I don't care what people suspect. If you do the job right, no one will connect it to me. I've heard enough excuses. It's time for results.'

Having given his orders, the rancher turned about and went back inside.

Missouri stood in the darkness seething with anger. Tony Santos never knew how close he had come to a knife in the back. Nobody spoke to Missouri Sam that way and lived. His professional pride dictated that he should kill Lawton and the homicidal madness slowly creeping into his brain was telling him that Jane too must die. Now his anger was tempting him to add Santos to his list.

Silently, the killer retraced his steps to the ruin where he was living. For a long while he sat in the darkness and brooded. Lately some of his former victims had been coming to him in his sleep and his rest was becoming increasingly troubled.

The rangers were out of bed early, feeding and saddling their horses before breakfast. They were not sure that they would be doing any riding but if horses were needed they would be needed in a hurry so the mounts had to be ready.

As the four men ate breakfast they planned their move against Dawson and his customers. They would approach the saloon, two from the front and two from the back at a time when the regular drinkers had assembled for their daily heart-starters. When they were sure that they had gleaned all possible information from that source, they would begin searching the ruins if such action was required.

Impatiently they waited, watching the saloon as the regular customers started arriving. Concealed in an upper room of the hotel, Jane and Ben watched the newcomers from a convenient window. Most lived in the immediate area and the girl knew them. She saw no strangers, only a couple of the local alcoholics who lived within a short ride of the town.

'If you want information from that crew,' Jane laughed, 'I suggest that you get into that saloon quickly while they are still able to talk.'

Ben agreed. Reluctant though he was to leave such charming company, he knew that the others would be keen to start the action. He went downstairs and for the last time ran through the plan of action.

He would take the back of the saloon with Harris. They would collect anyone sleeping in the shack behind the building and herd them into the bar. Marty and Bell would position themselves at the front door to prevent anyone leaving.

Harris would bring a sawn-off shotgun and Marty would carry his Winchester in case a long shot became necessary.

Then Ben told Shelley, 'Lock your doors and keep a gun handy. We can't be sure what's going to happen in the next half-hour or so. We'll call you when it's safe to open up again.'

Jane looked concerned and said anxiously, 'You be careful, Ben.'

'Time we got this party started,' Ben said, as he put on his hat and led the way out through the hotel's back door.

Peering through the broken roof, Missouri watched them go.

SEVENTEEN

It was Harris, the older ranger, who first saw something unusual. He pointed to the cottonwood branch hanging on the fence behind the saloon. 'Someone's been signalling someone else.'

Ben was not so sure. 'A branch on a fence don't mean much.'

'It does to me. During the war I was in a partisan unit for a while. A bush on a fence looks nothing unusual, but to those who knew, it was often a signal. Look at the distance that cottonwood tree is from the fence. The wind wouldn't carry that branch there. Someone put it there.'

They moved closer to the fence and the lanky ranger pointed to other dried pieces of foliage in the long grass. 'Someone has been meeting someone else here on more than one occasion. Now all we need to find is who needs to keep such meetings secret.'

Drawing his gun, Ben pushed open the door of the adobe shack. It was only two rooms with a couple of untidy bunks. They reeked of tobacco, spilled liquor and unwashed bodies but both were empty.

Cautiously they advanced to the saloon's back door with its split, weathered boards and peeling paint. After listening for a second, Ben tried the door. It was unlocked. The hinges creaked slightly as he opened the door but the sound of voices from the bar area on the other side of another door, drowned it out. The first room was a storage room. A door led out of this into living quarters, luckily unoccupied. Quickly crossing the room the pair paused at the door leading to the bar. Ben saw that his companion was ready and threw it open.

Dawson uttered a startled oath and reached beneath the bar for his shotgun but was too late.

'Rangers here,' Ben shouted. 'Nobody move.'

The twin muzzles of the shotgun that Harris held ready brought instant compliance with his order.

Simultaneously, Marty and Bell appeared at the front door.

Besides Dawson there were only Jasper, Santos and three others in the bar. The saloon owner snarled, 'What's going on, Lawton? You can't just bust into my place like that.'

Before the ranger could reply, the situation changed dramatically.

Harris immediately recognized Jasper. The muzzles of the gun swung toward him. 'Bill Jarvis, get your hands up.'

Jasper came backwards out of his chair, drawing

his gun as he rolled behind two drinkers seated nearby. The pair, well on the way to being drunk, seemed not to realize what was happening. They remained as if frozen in their seats until he thrust his gun between them and blasted a shot at Harris.

The tall ranger could not shoot back for fear that he might hit one of the pair who belatedly realized their peril.

Ben concentrated on the next most dangerous man in the room. Dawson had shot both hands skywards but Tony Santos, in a surge of alcoholic recklessness, had whipped out his six-gun and swung the muzzle at the ranger. Behind him Ben heard Jasper fire again but he only had eyes for Santos.

He squeezed the trigger and saw the big rancher flinch. Something whizzed past his face as a cloud of gunsmoke began filling the low-ceilinged room.

Marty had an unobstructed view of Jasper from the front door and fired one shot from his rifle as the gunman fired at Harris again. The bullet struck Jasper and shattered his thigh but the pain had not yet registered. Already crouched on the floor, the slug had not knocked him off his feet.

Ben and Santos fired almost together. The latter's shot did no damage, but the ranger saw a look of surprise appear on his opponent's battered features. He was about to fire again when Santos dropped his gun and fell to the floor.

As his human shields fled in opposite directions, Jasper raised himself for another shot at Harris but a blast of buckshot ripped through his throat and upper chest. Bleeding profusely, he fell forward onto his face. The lanky ranger saw no need to fire the second barrel. Blood from a bullet graze on his upper left arm showed that one of Jasper's shots had not missed by much.

'Watch the others!' Ben called, as he hurried to where Santos was writhing on the ground. A widening pool of blood near him showed that he was gravely wounded.

'Stay still, Santos, and I'll try to help.'

A blast of obscenity came back by way of reply. Then the dying man gasped, 'You can't help me – you badge-wearing sonofabitch.' The effort caused Santos to cough blood. 'Missouri—' he gasped.

'What about Missouri?'

But Tony Santos would never speak again. The life had gone from his wide-open eyes.

Ben stood up. 'Anyone hurt?'

Harris was rolling up his sleeve to examine the bullet graze. 'If Jarvis there was a little bit better shot I would have been.'

'What's the meaning of this?' Dawson was recovering from his fright.

Harris glared at him. 'That fella who started the shooting was an outlaw named Jarvis. He broke jail a couple of years ago and killed a sheriff's deputy who happened to be my brother. Jarvis and I are old enemies. I thought he was hiding out in Mexico somewhere. What were you doing sheltering him?'

The saloon owner knew that he could be in serious trouble and disclaimed all knowledge of the man's past. 'He came here looking for work about six months ago and I took him on. I didn't know anything about him being wanted by the law.' Dawson had lost all his bluster and now feared that he was about to be arrested. Very slowly he moved away from the gun under the bar and lowered his hands. He did not want any of his movements to be seen as threatening.

Quickly the rangers set about questioning the three customers. It did not take long to establish that Hank Gibbons and Elmer Blanche and Joe Moore were not connected with Missouri in any way. They had heard of him but that was all. Their major crime seemed to have been in developing a taste for Dawson's rotgut whiskey. All three were happy to depart the scene when they were allowed to go.

Dawson would not get off so lightly. When questioned about Missouri he seemed to know only of the man's reputation. After a series of questions, the rangers were convinced that he knew nothing or was a very good liar.

'Who was meeting who out back of the saloon?' Harris demanded.

The saloon keeper shook his head. 'I don't know. No one told me about any meetings and I sure as hell didn't see any.'

Ben tried a milder approach. He pointed out that Dawson could avoid being charged with harbouring a fugitive if he was prepared to co-operate. At first the man thought he had nothing to offer but then he had a flash of inspiration. 'It might have been Tony Santos. He didn't have a watch and a couple of times asked me to tell him when it was ten o'clock. At the right time he would go out that back door. He must have been meeting someone.'

'And you don't know who it was?' Ben asked.

'I don't know and never wanted to know. Tony was a dangerous man and I figured I was safest staying behind the bar and minding my own business.'

Missouri's secret was still safe.

Jane had been waiting anxiously after she heard the shooting. Finally her curiosity became too much. She unlocked the door and went out onto the hotel veranda. The gunshots had brought out Waldren, and Gonzales was also standing in the doorway of the ruin where he had been living.

Hank Gibbons was hurrying past but raised his hat when he saw the girl.

'Mr Gibbons,' she called, 'what's happening?'

The man paused and pointed back at Dawson's. 'There was all hell busted loose in there. The rangers killed Jasper and Tony Santos. Me and Elmer almost got shot ourselves. There was lead flying everywhere.'

'Were any of the rangers hurt?'

'The big, lanky one got a bullet graze on his arm but none of the others got hit.'

Missouri heard the exchange and decided that it was time to leave Red Rock Crossing. His employer was dead and no one would know that the legendary Missouri Sam, had failed. But to satisfy the demands of his own warped standards, two more people had to die. Those he had marked for death would go. None had escaped him yet. Although Missouri was becoming increasingly irrational, he knew that today was not the time for more killing.

He would leave, but return later in another guise when all the excitement had died down. The girl would still be at the hotel and Lawton, as a Texas ranger, would be easy to trace when he was ready.

Waldren was going to get his mule when he saw Jane on the veranda looking anxiously up the road towards the saloon. Her parents joined her as the preacher drew level. He remarked on the waste of lives and shook his head in despair. 'When will we learn?' he muttered.

Shelley agreed that it was not a good day. The recent bloodshed had him seriously thinking of moving away but who would buy a hotel beside an unpredictable river in a decaying town?

'I'll be moving on today,' Waldren announced. 'It seems I have had little enough effect around here. I thank you though for your friendship. The Shelley family will be a bright spot in my otherwise sad memories of this place.'

'Come around and see us when you are packed up,' Josh invited.

When Waldren went to collect his mule, he found Gonzales was there putting the bridle on his horse.

'Are you leaving too, Señor Gonzales?'

'*Sí.* My horse she is strong enough to travel again and I must go north to find work. No work for me here.'

Leading their animals, the pair walked together back to where they had been staying. There they found Ben and Marty waiting.

EIGHTEEN

'Going somewhere, gents?' Marty asked. Even as he spoke, the ranger suddenly had a new doubt. He had never considered that there could be more than one killer but now the possibility stared him in the face.

'We both reckon it's time we were moving,' Waldren answered.

Gonzales remained silent prepared to let the preacher act as spokesman.

'Both headed the same way?' Ben enquired casually.

The answers dispelled his latest doubt. The preacher was headed north to Three Mesas but Gonzales announced his intention of turning to the east along the north bank of the San Tomas where there were several ranches.

Waldren could tell that the rangers were not paying a social call. He looked shrewdly at Ben. 'You appear to have something on your mind, young man. What's troubling you?'

Ben answered. 'I'm afraid I'll have to search you

and Mr. Gonzales. As you know, there was some shooting at Dawson's and a couple of men were killed. The other rangers are still fixing loose ends over that at the saloon. You also know that there have been some strange things going on around here and we have reason to believe that a hired killer known as Missouri Sam has been in town.'

'And you think that this man could be one of us?'

'We don't know what to think, but you and Gonzales here have both been in the area at the same time and we have to include you in our list of suspects. If we can get you off that list it gives us more time to follow up a few more leads.' As he spoke Ben felt that Waldren knew that they had no other real leads.

The preacher smiled. 'You can do what you want to satisfy yourself about me. I will co-operate fully. I'm sure the good Lord meant us to help lawful authority.'

When Ben turned to Gonzales, the Mexican shrugged his shoulders. 'I am hiding nothing. What do you want me to do?'

'We are interested in any weapons you have and would like to see what you are packing to take with you.'

The Mexican pulled aside his serape to disclose the revolver on his belt. 'I have this gun but have not fired it for a long time and I have my shotgun that you have seen.'

Ben plucked the Colt from its holster and sniffed

the barrel. It was clean and well-oiled. He knew that Pedro had been shot with a .38 but the cartridge was a common one and many Navy Colts similar to the Mexican's had been converted to fire it. Together they went into the ruined building where Gonzales had stored his meagre belongings with the smaller items in a pair of battered saddle-bags. Apart from blankets and clothing and rudimentary eating utensils there were only a few revolver bullets and a box three parts filled with shotgun cartridges. The Mexican gave an account of his recent movements and they would be easy to check later. He was philosophical about being under suspicion and though he probably resented being searched, he did not object. Ben still had misgivings but could see no reason to delay him any longer. If he was hoping that Marty might find something, he was disappointed.

Marty had searched Waldren and he, too, had found nothing suspicious. The preacher's only weapon was a double-barrelled, 10-gauge shotgun.

Neither had a .44/40 rifle or ammunition. Nor did they have much money and a high-priced killer like Missouri could be expected to demonstrate some signs of affluence.

Trying to hide their disappointment, the rangers chatted to the pair as they saddled their animals. Ben had hoped that the unexpected search might have thrown up some sort of evidence but the plan had failed. If Missouri was one of these men, he had covered his tracks well.

Being a keen horseman, Ben noticed that Gonzales's grey horse was a better animal than a casual glance would reveal. Its grooming had been neglected and ungroomed greys seemed to look worse than other colours. The hacked about mess of its mane and tail did nothing for the animal's looks but it had no conformation faults when its appearance was closely examined.

'That's not a bad horse, Gonzales. What happened to make such a mess of its mane and tail?'

The Mexican smiled ruefully. 'One night I put him in a corral with a skinny little Indian mustang. That mustang, she is hungry and chew my horse's mane and tail. It spoil his looks but he is still a good horse.'

'He looks it,' the ranger agreed.

The rangers wished the travellers well and started back to Dawson's saloon to see if they could help the others. Both men were beset by doubts as they strongly suspected that Missouri was either Waldren or Gonzales but with no evidence they could not detain either.

Gonzales trotted past them heading for the crossing but Waldren hitched his mule outside the hotel. He was saying goodbye to the Shelley family. Later he emerged clutching a sizeable packed lunch that Jane had insisted on preparing for him.

Thanking the Shelleys profusely and wishing them well, the preacher climbed onto his mule and turned it towards the crossing.

Josh was secretly pleased to see Waldren go as he

considered him a nuisance but as Jane looked after the retreating figure she said, 'I'll miss him. He was a funny sort of preacher but I feel he was a good man.'

Her father shook his head doubtfully. 'I'm still not sure about him. There's something not quite right about him. He seems too good to be true.'

'I think he practises better than he preaches,' Jane said.

'I think Ben Lawton suspected that Waldren might have been the man who gave you such a scare and may even have killed Pedro.'

The girl scoffed at the idea. 'Preacher Waldren had a stiff, rather awkward way of walking. The man I saw could move like a cat.'

'Did you tell Ben that?'

'I might have. He's been very busy of late and though he's here at the crossing, I have not seen as much of him as I thought I would.'

The rangers had finished their work at Dawson's and were looking forward to a brief period of relaxation but Ben had other ideas. The thought that a killer might be riding away made him frustrated and restless. His stay at Red Rock Crossing had not been a good period for law and order. There had been two unsolved murders, his partner had been injured, he had been forced to shoot his prisoner and other men had died in what seemed to be unrelated gunfights.

Rather than admit defeat he suggested a search of the ruins. Four men had a better chance of finding

142

something than two. Reluctantly the others agreed.

An hour later they had found rats, spiders, rubbish and Bell had even been forced to kill a snake but real evidence seemed to have eluded them. They were comparing notes in the ruin where Gonzales had been living and were about to abandon their efforts when Harris glanced up at the exposed rafters. Because he was taller than the others and the light was shining through the broken roof at the right angle, he noticed something on the rafter over his head. 'There's something up there,' he told the others.

On closer examination, the dust on that part of the rafter had been wiped away as if by something passing over it. Curious, but not really expecting to find much, the lanky ranger jumped up and grabbed the rafter, intending to pull himself up high enough to see what was on it. Instead, he dislodged a small black bundle and what looked like a metal pipe that fell to the ground with a loud clang.

Ben picked up the bundle. It appeared to be black cloth wrapped around a small, heavy, cardboard box. As he unwrapped the cloth, he saw that holes had been cut in it. 'It looks like Missouri has left his mask behind,' he said.

With the others crowding around, he opened the box. It bore the label of the Winchester Repeating Arms Company and was not quite full but contained .44/40 cartridges.

Bell had picked up the metal pipe and was examining it curiously. It was less than two feet long and had one thick end and a couple of flanges along its length. When he looked through the hole in the centre of the pipe he said in surprise, 'This looks like some kind of rifle barrel.'

Ben took the object from his comrade's hand and studied it a moment. 'I saw one of these gadgets before in a gunsmith's shop. It's called an adapter. He reckoned they were common in Europe but never really took on here. It's a rifle barrel made to fit inside a shotgun barrel. I think we'll find that the thick end of this gadget fits neatly into the firing chamber of a twelve-gauge shotgun.' He took a .44/40 bullet from the box and it fitted perfectly into the chamber of the adapter. 'We were looking for a Winchester repeater, but Missouri was using the same cartridges in a single-shot weapon. Now I know why Gonzales had rifle sights on his shotgun. He had a few lead slugs for appearance's sake but his shotgun could be turned into a rifle. I know now that Gonzales or Missouri, whoever he is, killed Grant and fired the shot aimed for me, that killed Hamel's man, Martin, by accident. When things went wrong, he fired one more shot through the adapter, slipped it out and probably hid it under his serape, then fired a shot through the shotgun barrel. When he told me that he had swapped shots with the shooter, I fell for his story. There's no doubt. Gonzales is Missouri.'

'But why would he leave such a damning piece of evidence behind?' Marty asked.

'He had no choice. You and I were there when he was packing up and he knew he was under suspicion. It was safer to get out of town as quickly as possible and hope that the adapter and cartridges would not be found for a long time. I thought we were wasting our time but our little search stopped Missouri from carrying away the evidence. We've got him.' Ben could not conceal his elation. 'We have the proof we need. Let's get our horses. We're going after Missouri Sam.'

NINETEEN

The four riders splashed across the San Tomas and followed the recent tracks along the trail to Three Mesas. For some distance it appeared that Waldren and Gonzales had both gone the same way, but after the climb out of the river valley the horse's tracks swung to the east. The hoofprints were wider apart and deeper as Missouri urged his mount to greater speed.

He had an hour's start and, at the pace he was travelling, the hunters estimated that he was somewhere between eight and nine miles ahead. The country was mostly open with wide expanses of grey-blue sagebrush, broken occasionally by darker green belts of mesquite. The red soil was soft and retained clear tracks so the rangers urged their mounts to a canter in the hope of closing the distance between them and their quarry. A long stretch of rising ground ahead limited visibility so taking a short cut was out of the question. They had to stay on the tracks.

At a point on a high ridge, the party halted. Harris

produced a pair of field-glasses and studied the scene ahead. The country had changed. Before them lay miles of mesquite-covered plain, deeply scored in places by erosion gullies. It would be hard to make any real speed in such country.

'I thought I saw dust over there,' Harris said, and pointed towards a distant butte. 'Can't see it now though.'

Bell stood in his stirrups and looked ahead. A smile, partially hidden by his large moustache, appeared on his face. 'I know this country. If he's over there, he's headed into a big loop in the San Tomas. He'll have to swing away to the north to get out of it. If we don't go in there we'll gain a mile or two on him.'

'We won't if he decides to cross back over the river again,' Marty reminded him.

'He can't. The river there is in a deep gorge. He can't get down to it with a horse.'

Missouri stopped a while to rest his horse and cursed the barren country around him, He had lost count of the number of deeply eroded gullies he had crossed. Several he followed hoping they would give him a gradual descent to the river but all ended in sheer drops. Each fruitless diversion was taking time and helping to tire his horse. He had arrived at Red Rock Crossing via the road from Three Mesas but on the return journey he decided to give the town a wide berth. If any lawmen were on his trail and were hoping to save time, they would be likely to head for there. Being unfamiliar with the country, he had not known about the meandering canyon cut by the river. It worried him a little that if the rangers were tracking him, they might have the advantage of local knowledge and might short-cut his path rather than rely upon following his tracks. But remembering the puzzled looks on the rangers' faces back at the crossing he was not even sure that he would be pursued.

By force of habit, Missouri always rested where he had a good view of the surrounding countryside. He rolled a cigarette and sat in the shade of a high boulder and took in the scenery. Then, away to the west, the sun flashed briefly on metal. It was time to go. Away from the road in an area devoid of livestock the only people likely to be in the locality would be those hunting him. They were still a long way away and, as he tightened his saddle cinch again, the gunman saw no cause for alarm. He had tricks that he had not tried yet but first he would swing to the north to avoid completely the winding river that had caused him so many problems.

'Our horses are tiring,' Harris said, touching the spur to his sweat-caked bay as it climbed out of yet another arroyo. 'We've used them pretty hard the last couple of days and this broken country is knocking hell out of them.'

'We ain't never gonna catch up with that *hombre*,' Bell complained.

'I think we might,' Ben said. 'My horse has had plenty of rest and is full of hard feed. If I take a short cut and ride him hard, I might be able to cut Missouri off. If you *hombres* stay on his tracks, he won't be able to double back. I'll take him if he walks into me or pick up his tracks if he has already gone past.'

'Be careful,' Marty warned. 'If the stories they tell are half right, Missouri's a bad man to tackle on your own.'

'If he gets a bit hard to handle I'll try to pin him down and hold him in place until the rest of you come up,' Ben assured him. He turned to Bell. 'What's the general direction I need to ride to get ahead of someone trying to get out of the loop of the river?'

The other ranger studied the eastern skyline for a while and finally indicated a rocky spire. 'That's not far from where the river bends again and heads east. Get yourself over there slightly north of that pointed rock because if we have guessed right, he'll be going past there. You should see him or his tracks.'

Ben turned the chestnut's head to the north. 'I'll see you in a couple of hours. If you hear shooting, come as quickly as you can.'

He rode hard but varied the pace according to the ground. Sometimes he trotted, at other times he cantered and, where the ground allowed, galloped for short stretches. By constantly changing the pace, he avoided the long sustained burst of galloping that

149

tired horses very quickly. The horse was well-bred and willing and nearly a week on hard feed had given it plenty of energy. It was also sure-footed and could maintain a good pace even in rough ground.

The miles rolled behind them. The chestnut's neck and quarters were lathered with foam but, true to its breeding, the horse responded whenever an increase in pace was needed. Dust rose behind them but Ben was counting on the broken nature of the country to conceal his presence. He did not want to run into an ambush that Missouri might arrange for his hunters.

It would not have helped the ranger's peace of mind to know that his quarry had already detected his presence. Missouri's horse had travelled many unnecessary miles because its rider was unfamiliar with the country and was starting to tire. During one of his rest breaks the killer had glimpsed dust on his back trail and knew by the small cloud that it was made only by one rider. That person was sure to cut his tracks soon and would start following them. If he could trap the single hunter, he would gain an extra horse and probably a much-needed rifle. His anger flared again when he remembered the adapter he had been forced to leave behind. He would need to lure his victim into fairly close range and rely upon his shotgun and revolver. It would be fatal to create a situation where a lawman could keep him pinned down by long-range rifle fire. He would need to create a situation where he held all the aces.

Remounting the tired grey, he pushed on and covered another mile before he found the place that he sought.

It was a wide expanse of barren red earth ending in a thin belt of mesquite with a few rocks scattered around, the sort of place where an ambusher might await his victim. He wanted the ranger watching that spot because he would not be there. On one side of the open area, about halfway across, there were a couple of small rocks and a few thin bushes; not much cover but good enough for someone who knew how to hide, especially if his target was looking the other way.

First he had to arrange the bait. He tied his mount in the mesquite where a man who was looking hard, would catch a glimpse of it through the foliage. Then he removed the striped Mexican serape and the big sombrero. Fifty yards from the horse he arranged them behind some rocks in such a way that an alert man might catch sight of small pieces of his outfit. The ranger would be looking for a sombrero and a serape and he would not be disappointed. But nothing must be too obvious. The lawman would know that he was not hunting a careless man and would be suspicious if he saw the bait too easily.

Finally he went to his ambush position. By using his knife and moving a couple of small rocks, he was able to scratch a shallow trench in the loose soil. Screened by a clump of stunted greasewood, he arranged his shotgun ammunition close at hand and stretched out with the gun sighted between a couple of low rocks. He threw a couple of handfuls of loose dust over his clothing the better to blend with his surroundings. Opening the gun, he slipped in a solid lead slug and settled down to wait.

It was far from comfortable in the burning sun without a hat and Missouri hoped that his wait would not be a long one.

It wasn't.

TWENTY

Ben knew when he found Missouri's tracks that his man was ahead of him. He could also see by the occasional dragged hoofmark that although the grey horse was moving at a smart trot, it was tiring. Only a man who knew he was being pursued would push his mount so hard in the heat.

The ranger had chased enough Comanche and Kiowa raiders to know that smart men continually checked to see who was following and under the right circumstances, often turned on their pursuers. He had no doubt that Missouri was aware that he was being followed.

Alarm bells rang in his brain when he saw the fugitive's tracks showing so clearly across the bare clay pan ahead. It was as though Missouri wanted him to follow them. Some instinct told him that the landscape before him was not as harmless as it seemed.

Halfway across the open ground, Ben checked his

mount and looked around. He knew that Missouri had no rifle and chose to stay clear of the mesquite ahead until he was sure it was safe. He rode a little closer and then something caught his eye, just a glimpse of white showing through a slight break in the mesquite. Immediately he knew that it was Missouri's grey horse. Where was its rider?

Drawing his Winchester from its saddle scabbard, Ben halted his mount again and studied the bushes ahead. Aware that the gunman only had short-range weapons, he felt that it was safe to stop in the open and look. Then he saw what he had hoped to see, part of the gunman's dark brown sombrero and just the corner of a red-striped serape showing around the edge of a boulder.

Sixty yards to the ranger's right, Missouri carefully lined his sights on his pursuer who was obligingly sitting still. With a feeling of satisfaction, he squeezed the trigger and felt the gun kick hard against his shoulder.

Ben heard the report of the gun and felt the hot breath as the heavy lead ball whizzed past his face. Instinctively he glanced to the right and saw a cloud of powdersmoke hanging over a greasewood bush. Somehow Missouri had missed what should have been an easy shot. But he would reload quickly and the second time the shooter might have more luck.

Touching the spurs to his mount, Ben raced it forward. The move caught Missouri by surprise because he knew that most men in similar situations tried to turn back. When he tried to swing his gun to the right, one of the sheltering boulders was in his way. Cursing, he rose to his knees and fired over the rock but Ben was already out of accurate range. Worse still, he had now cut Missouri off from his horse. Almost in despair the gunman fired a third time, but the shot missed again and he heard the deformed slug whine off a rock about a foot from his target.

Ben came out of his saddle, hitting the ground running and jumped behind the nearest boulder. Taking advantage of the break caused by Missouri's need to reload, he raised the rifle and raked the ambusher's position with four rapid shots.

The bullets raised a cloud of red dust around the target and one grazed the calf of Missouri's leg. The gunman could only keep under cover and curse his luck. Any movement brought a rifle bullet that struck within inches of where he was sheltering. It was only a matter of time before the ranger got everything right and he was hit.

'Throw your guns out, Missouri,' Ben called. 'You can't get away and three more rangers will be here soon.'

The gunman played for time as he glanced around himself for an escape route. He saw his best option, a shallow ditch a few yards behind where he was lying. It wound its way towards a clump of stunted trees where the cover looked better than his present position. Missouri decided to delay matters as he reloaded his shotgun.

He shouted back. 'How do I know you won't kill me if I give up?' The fake Mexican accent was gone.

'I swear I won't shoot if you throw out your weapons,' Ben answered.

'Just wait—' Having allayed the ranger's suspicions slightly, Missouri made his move. Springing to his feet, he launched himself over a few yards of dirt to land face-down in the ditch. As he hit the ground a rifle bullet sprayed dust in his face but he wriggled forward trying to keep as low as he could.

Guessing his opponent's intention, Ben threw caution to the wind and ran towards him firing his rifle as he came. He was within thirty yards of Missouri when his rifle clicked empty. There was no time to reload.

Missouri heard the running footsteps and came up to his knees just as Ben was drawing his Colt. The ranger saw the muzzle of the shotgun swing toward him as he brought up his own weapon. Hoping that Missouri was still firing slugs, he jumped frantically to the side. At that range even light shot could be fatal.

The gunman's shot was instinctive rather than aimed and he was panting and firing from an unbalanced position. Again it missed. Throwing aside the empty gun Missouri drew his revolver but Ben had a slight advantage and got his shot away first. The bullet struck the kneeling gunman twisting him sideways as he fell back to the ground. But with lightning reflexes, he flipped onto his back and was bringing his Colt up again.

Ben did not hesitate. He triggered two more quick shots into the man on the ground and was prepared to fire again until he saw the revolver fall from Missouri's hand.

Ashen-faced, with his shirt front bloody he struggled to breathe, but could not speak. While life remained in him, he glared at the ranger for a second or two and then the baleful stare became fixed in death.

By force of habit, Ben reloaded his gun and was just about to search the dead man when he heard pounding hoofs and his comrades burst out of the brush spurring their lathered mounts towards him.

Marty hauled his mare to a stop and jumped from the saddle. 'We came as quick as we could. Are you OK?'

'I am now but he nearly got me. If he'd had a rifle I would have been a gone goose. He got a clear shot at me with a solid lead slug and missed.'

'From what I heard of this back-shooting skunk, he don't miss very often,' Harris observed.

'It was his gun that was the trouble.' Ben picked it up as he spoke and pointed to the sights. 'These sights are for a .44/40 bullet coming out of a rifled barrel. They didn't have a lot of relevance to a lead ball coming out of a smooth bore. Without the adapter this gun was only as accurate as an old musket and I never saw one of them that shot straight.'

'You were lucky,' Bell said.

'I know it,' Ben admitted. 'He outsmarted me but his gun was not good enough.'

'Any idea who he is – or was?' Marty asked.

Ben shook his head. 'He's not a Mexican. He spoke when I tried to talk him into surrendering.'

'He had me fooled,' Marty told them.

'He fooled us all,' Ben said. 'He was very good at fooling people and that's why he lasted so long.'

Later they searched Missouri and his belongings. In a carefully concealed pocket in a saddle-bag they found a bundle of large denomination notes and a couple of letters addressed to a certain Emile Brock in New Orleans. One was written by Tony Santos asking him to do some unspecified work for him. The rangers were sure then that they could connect both Santos and Missouri to Grant's murder. All agreed that Pedro had been killed when he accidentally stumbled upon Missouri stalking one of his intended victims.

The rangers' next task was to deliver the body to the sheriff at Three Mesas, wire through a report to their captain and, unless instructed otherwise, return to their camp.

Ben was looking forward to the return journey. Unless something unforeseen happened, he intended going back by way of Red Rock Crossing. His partners might return by the main road as there was nothing in the crossing to attract them. Ben could understand that. He also had seen plenty of towns that he liked more, but had never seen a girl he liked as much as Jane Shelley.